CONTEMPORARY AMERICAN FICTION

THE DEATH OF JIM LONEY

James Welch is an American Indian—Blackfeet and Gros Ventre. He attended schools on the Blackfeet and Fort Belknap reservations in Montana; he graduated from the University of Montana, where he studied writing with the late Richard Hugo. He is the author of two other highly acclaimed novels—*Winter in the Blood* (1974) and *Fools Crow* (1986)—both of which are available in the Penguin Contemporary American Fiction series.

THE DEATH OF JIM LONEY

JAMES WELCH

PENGUIN BOOKS

PENGUIN BOOKS
Viking Penguin Inc., 40 West 23rd Street,
New York, New York 10010, U.S.A.
Penguin Books Ltd, 27 Wrights Lane, London W8 5TZ
(Publishing & Editorial) and Harmondsworth,
Middlesex, England (Distribution & Warehouse)
Penguin Books Australia Ltd, Ringwood,
Victoria, Australia
Penguin Books Canada Limited, 2801 John Street,
Markham, Ontario, Canada L3R 1B4
Penguin Books (N.Z.) Ltd, 182–190 Wairau Road,
Auckland 10, New Zealand

First published in the United States of America by
Harper & Row, Publishers, Inc. 1979
Published in Penguin Books 1987

LIBRARY OF CONGRESS CATALOGING IN PUBLICATION DATA
Welch, James, 1940–
The death of Jim Loney.
(Contemporary American fiction)
I. Title. II. Series.
[PS3573.E44D44 1987] 813'.54 87-8613
ISBN 0 14 01.0291 4

Printed in the United States of America by
R. R. Donnelley & Sons Company, Harrisonburg, Virginia
Set in Caledonia

Ah, to have a horse, and gallop away,
singing, away to someone you loved
perhaps, into the heart of all the
simplicity and peace in the world;
was not that like the opportunity
afforded man by life itself?

Malcolm Lowry,
Under the Volcano

1

Loney watched the muddy boys bang against each other and he thought of a passage from the Bible: "Turn away from man in whose nostrils is breath, for of what account is he?" The boys stood up, some walking back to the huddle, others standing with hands on hips and heads bent. The rain fell, but more lightly now. Beyond the arc lights the world was black. The shiny helmets lined up against each other and crashed again, this time a little farther downfield. A couple of car horns honked. Loney could remember no other passages and he was surprised that he had remembered that one.

It had been a good game until the rain came, somewhere in the third quarter. It was the second rain of the day and it had wiped out the tender autumn field.

"That boy can run," said the man next to him. "He's a regular horse, that one!"

"No lie!" said another. "Who is that?"

"I can't tell his number."

"It's Eckland," said the first man.

Loney stepped forward and squinted through the pale light. The men were not talking to him but that was all right. The rain was not cold.

"How many time-outs we got left?"

A wispy little man pulled a note pad out of his pocket. "We're out. They've got two left."

"Goddamn it, Carl, what did you have to tell me that for?"

"We're shit out of luck. What can you do in forty seconds?"

"That's a lot of time, Harve. You'd be surprised."

Loney looked at the scoreboard: 13–6. A touchdown and extra point would tie it up. It looked like Harlem would get the touchdown. They were near the goal line. Then they were in and the car horns sounded and the clock stopped. Across the field the cheerleaders, holding a long piece of plastic over their heads, kicked and danced. A tall thin player raced out onto the field holding a kicking tee. He wore one black shoe and one white shoe. His uniform was spotless.

"Oh, my dying ass. They're going to kick the goddamn thing."

"You'd be surprised, Harve. I smell a fish in the barrel."

"Can it, pint-size. I know what I see."

"Who is that?"

"Young Cutler."

"Oh, shit—oh, dear."

But it was a fake kick. The holder scooped the ball off the ground and started to circle right. The kicker followed him, dancing behind him like a thin bird. The Chinook players fell back from the line to cover the end zone. Suddenly the holder stopped and cocked his arm and the thin player ran into him. The ball seemed to hang in the air as both players fell to the muddy field; then it, too, fell, landing on the thin player's back. He rolled over, pulled the ball into his midsection and lay there without moving.

Loney glanced at Harve, but Harve had one big farmer's hand covering his face. He hadn't seen a thing. He looked like a man at a funeral.

2

Loney walked through the smoky night. Away from the people and the lights, the rain was colder. He moved his shoulders up and down to make them warm. He stopped and lit a cigarette and glanced back toward the field. The banks of lights had been turned off and Loney could hear the noise of car motors racing. He lived two blocks from the football field and he smelled the smoke from the wood stoves banked against the night and the rain.

Four cars speeded by, horns honking, people yelling. A girl leaned out the window of a pickup and screamed, "Go, Big Orange!"

It was the first week of October and the rain had been falling for three days without letup. Before that, there had been one clear day, and before that, a long week of rain. Loney had been working for a farmer out north, helping with the summer-fallowing, but the rain had wiped them out and he didn't mind. That one clear day the farmer had come to Loney's house and told him to come to work the next day. But when it rained again, Loney sat at his kitchen table and watched it. He had made enough from harvesting to keep himself for a while. His needs were few and not great in his mind.

It was early and Loney did not want to go home. He wanted to go downtown for a drink. But because he didn't go out much anymore he had to stop and decide where to drink. He was a block from the bars and the rain had soaked through his shoes. For a moment he thought of giving up the idea. He had a bottle of wine at home, but he wanted a drink of whiskey, a drink that would warm him inside and out. He decided on Kennedy's, but his father might be there, so he settled on the Serviceman's.

As he walked toward the lights, he thought again of the Bible passage. He hadn't read the Bible in fifteen years. He wondered why he had remembered that particular passage. Did it have to do with the players, the people around him, himself? He decided the passage was wrong, he had gotten it wrong. There was no sense to it.

He walked and he realized that he was seeing things strangely, and he remembered that it had been that way at the football game. It was as though he were exhausted and drowsy, but his head was clear. He was aware of things around him—the shadowy trees, the glistening sidewalk, the dark cat that moved into the dark. The wood smoke had been with him for days and he felt drowsy on it and he smelled the wet leaves in the gutter. He saw and smelled these things and his head felt light, and he thought, I hear nothing, it is as quiet as death, and he did not hear the rain. The rain did not make a sound as it fell. The night glistened with the smell of wood smoke.

3

The bar was full but not packed. And it was quiet for ten o'clock on a Friday night. Loney felt awkward as he made his way down the bar. A young couple glanced in his direction, their faces blank with indifference. He found an empty stool beside the man and slid onto it.

The bartender, a lanky Indian named Russell, looked at him while he wiped his hands on a bar rag. "The Lone Ranger," he said.

"What's up?" said Loney.

"Business as usual. Trying to keep the women happy."

"It's tough," said Loney.

"What's your pleasure?"

"Bourbon—with a little water."

"You're coming up in the world."

Loney rubbed his forehead. It was wet. He settled down and waited for his drink. He hadn't been in the Serviceman's since last June, since Chuckwagon Days, when the fat government worker got thrown through the plate-glass window. The window was still gone, replaced by a large sheet of plywood. Someone had scrawled in lipstick: SLOW ME DOWN LORD.

Russell set Loney's drink on the bar. He had been a drinking acquaintance a few years ago, but that was history. Now is now, thought Loney, and he drank half the drink. It was almost pure bourbon.

"How's that?" said Russell.

Loney sat up straight and lowered his head, waiting for the burning knot to settle in his stomach. Then he swallowed and reached into his breast pocket for his cigarettes.

Russell wiped his hands on the bar rag and watched him. "You want some water?"

"It's fine. Jesus Christ, it's all right now."

Russell laughed. He didn't like Loney. He had never liked him and he could not say why. Even when they used to drink together he hadn't liked Loney and it always puzzled him. If it had been a woman, if we had fought over a woman, Russell thought, I could understand that. But it had never been a woman. When they drank together, they drank as men do who do not like each other. They drank quietly but tensely, neither of them wishing the other ill or well, only survival until next time. The only time a woman had been involved Russell had won. He took the woman home and fucked her. But even then he felt that he had been given her, that Loney hadn't cared one way or another. And maybe that was what he hated in Loney, the fact that he didn't seem to care. Russell, in his victory, had been made foolish.

But Loney had never really done anything to him, and right

now Russell could almost pity the poor bedraggled bastard trying to light a cigarette with a book of wet matches. He leaned over the bar and struck his Zippo. "You been to the football game?"

Loney sucked in his smoke and nodded.

"How bad was it?"

"Thirteen to twelve."

"Theirs?"

"Yes."

"Hell, that's a moral victory. Your goddamn right."

"Skin you."

"Skin you too."

They both laughed. It was an Indian joke.

"What have you been up to?" said Loney. He wiped his wet hair back away from his forehead.

"Eating the wife's cooking, getting fat." Russell bounced a fist off his flat belly. "You know I got married? Estelle Pipe? Almost a year now."

"Congratulations."

"You should try it."

"I just might."

"Keep your hands off your meat. Best year of my life."

"Congratulations."

"You got a woman?"

"Yes."

"Really?"

Loney nodded.

"What's her name? Do I know her?"

"No, you wouldn't know her."

"Why not?"

"She doesn't come in here."

"What's the matter with this place?"

"She's a schoolteacher."

"Ohhh." But Russell didn't believe him. He didn't believe Loney had a woman and it irritated him. "I hear from Sylvester that you're working for old Gronabeck."

"I was, until this rain got the best of us." Loney felt about ready to try the bourbon again.

"You should get a real job."

"That's the truth."

"You should work it for a while instead of sitting on it."

"Maybe." Loney lifted his eyebrows.

And Russell felt a little sorry for him. "Working for them farmers ain't so bad. You can't beat the hours."

Loney laughed and swallowed the whiskey. Russell laughed too. He could buy him a drink now. We're neither of us bad guys; just adversaries, that's all.

In the Serviceman's that night, nobody was bad and the night turned noisy and incidental to the long run.

4

Rhea rolled over onto her back and sighed, and the sun filled the room. It took her a moment to realize that today was Saturday and she had made it through another week. She began to feel the possibility of spirit again. It had been a long time; not a bad time, just a vaguely discontented time. The malaise had fallen over her like a patch of winter fog and she thought it had to do with the onset of winter in a cold country. But yesterday's snow had lifted her and at the same time had prepared her for the unruly months ahead, and today's sun burned away the traces of her malaise. She felt resolutely human.

She studied the picture on the wall above her bed. It was a print of a painting of a girl with orange hair and black dress. She often glanced at it in the morning, but this early sun threw a rare light on it and she decided it must be true. The man who had presented it to her had said the girl looked just like her. Today, for the first time, the long neck, the slender face, even the hair, although the wrong color, seemed much like her own. It was in the eyes that she found a resemblance that mystified her. There was something Oriental about the eyes and she had never thought of her own eyes that way. Moreover, the eyes were dark, opaque, while her own eyes were green and deep. Lively, she thought. Why do they always paint such passionless women? But I have been passionless the last few weeks. Maybe that's the resemblance. Two passionless women waiting for something to happen.

The clock/radio said 9:03. She walked into the bathroom and turned on the light above the mirror. Without her lipstick, her eye shadow and mascara, she looked less like the girl than she had imagined. She began to take off her nightgown to look at her body, but she thought, This is silly; a girl on a piece of pasteboard is making me do this. Still, she moved her gown to one side so she could see her shoulder and it was smooth and white and did look a little like the girl's one visible slightly rounded shoulder. She made a face. At least I have passion in me. And big white teeth. I could bite through a tree. "Grrr," she said. It always surprised her when friends, men especially, told her she had wonderful teeth. She always felt they were much too large for her mouth. And a little crooked. Sometimes when she listened to a person talk directly to her, she felt her lips pulling apart and she became conscious of her teeth and she couldn't concentrate on the words. At best, she thought her teeth were eccentric.

"I'm twenty-nine years old," she said as she ran the washcloth over her face.

She slipped into her robe and walked to the kitchen to put on her tea water. Then she went to the front door for the newspaper. The street was already black and drying in spots. What a strange country.

And she thought of the day before. That late afternoon she had been visiting Loney in his house, scolding him really, for she had found him drinking wine and half drunk. He would say nothing to her and she had decided to leave, perhaps for good, when she looked out the kitchen window and saw the thick heavy flakes. She had blurted, "Oh, look!" and together they watched through the window the snow turning blue in the dusk. She heard again the ticking clock as she ran her fingers through his hair. And she remembered the yellow stucco Catholic church across the street, as large and ominous as a ship on a swell. And the four box elders on the boulevard twisting darkly to the gray sky. Rhea had watched the first snow of the year drift and cover everything small and she thought she had never seen anything lovelier.

Now she touched her blond hair, cut as short and almost in the same style as Loney's, and the disappointment of seeing the first snow running down the gutter was tempered by the brilliant sun and the raw noise of a magpie in a tree across the street.

She fixed her tea and toasted an English muffin and carried them into the living room, where she sat down on the rug in a square of sunlight. She opened the paper to the weather section and ran her finger down the column of cities until she came to Dallas: 82° and 63°. That was warm for this time of year. She tried to imagine what her parents were doing right now. They would have finished breakfast hours ago. They got up at dawn every day. Saturday. Her father would probably be out shooting clay pigeons. A dumb sport. And her mother? Perhaps sitting in the sun reading the newspaper, or working on one of her splashy watercolors.

Most mornings when she read the Dallas weather, Rhea longed for those hot dry days, those empty afternoons of sunning or shopping or driving to Fort Worth and her grandmother's estate. She loved Fort Worth. It had a personality, with its old buildings, the cattleyards and the museums.

Rhea sipped her tea and looked out the sliding glass doors that opened onto a small deck. She remembered the last exhibit she had attended in an annex of the Amon Carter Museum. It was an exhibition of modern cowboy art, mostly plastic art. Most of the pieces were funny and quite serious, but she liked the saloon the best. It was a real saloon and you walked through the rough swinging doors and found yourself in another world. She smelled the manure and she stared at the red neon heart blinking in the dark above the bar. She heard the lonesome moan of a broken-hearted cowboy on the jukebox. There were bottles of Lone Star and Pearl beer and ashtrays full of cigarette butts on the bar, and in the corner, a rumpled bed with a big pile of dirt in the middle. She and her friend, whom she had thought she loved at the time, became silent as they allowed the music and manure to fill their senses. Then they looked at each other and laughed. They laughed until they were breathless, and then they hugged and Rhea had thought her life was perfect in that moment.

But when they walked out into the white light of the museum hall, an old dissatisfaction hit her like a mistral wind and she felt quite empty. She had felt it for some time, since receiving her M.A. from Southern Methodist that spring. She had no idea what she was going to use it for.

She looked at her plate. She hadn't touched her English muffin and the butter had made it soggy. She stood and walked into the kitchen. The carpet was warm from the sunlight. She found some cigarettes in a drawer and took one. She hardly ever smoked, but her memories had made her antsy.

Back in the living room she lit the cigarette with a large crystal lighter. And she remembered the professor, an assistant professor of literature, who had told her all about Montana. He had spent his summers in Montana since he was a kid. At the family place on Flathead Lake. He had told Rhea about the blue mountains, the green rivers, the small summer theater in Bigfork, and Glacier Park. He had given her an address in Helena where she could find out about teaching positions. Although they were the most casual of acquaintances, he had sensed her dissatisfaction. And so she wrote. And here she was. And she had been here two years. But instead of summer theaters and mountains and Glacier Park, she found herself in country that was all sky and flat land. She was in Big Sky country. With a vengeance. If it weren't for the Little Rockies and the Bearpaws, small mountains to the south of Harlem, there would be nothing to break the tan and blue horizon. As for summer theater, there was a movie house that showed Walt Disney and adventure films. It wasn't the end of the world, her grandmother would have said, but you could see it from here. But she said that about Fort Worth.

Rhea lay back and closed her eyes. The sun was grand and she hoped that Loney would be in shape today. She listened to the snow drip on the small deck. It was Saturday and sunny and Rhea felt the possibility of spirit again, an anticipation of something about to happen.

5

Loney was combing his hair when he heard the knocking. He put the hair oil in the medicine chest and turned out the light. The bathroom was on the dark side of the house.

He opened the back door and Rhea stood with her hands on her hips. "What's the meaning of this?" she said, gesturing with her head at the garbage can. It had been tipped over and a trail of trash led around the side of the house.

He frowned. "Goddamn dogs," he said.

"You should speak kindlier of them, you beast."

"Turdhounds," said Loney.

"You're an ugly one."

"Come in." He stood aside and let her pass.

"Oh, my! What have you done? It's so spotless!" Rhea walked around the kitchen, running her finger over the counters and shelves, looking into corners and under the table. "Oh, my, who's your decorator? I must have him!"

"Charles—Charles of Harlem." But Loney was happy and shy. "Would you like some coffee? It's only instant."

But Rhea continued to walk a tight circle in the small kitchen. She seemed to be searching for something. At last her eyes lit on him. "And look at you! You combed your hair. And shaved." She put her hand to her chest. "And did you bathe?"

Loney nodded. Her soft Southern voice had become a song and it confused him. He didn't know whether she was mocking him or not. Either way he didn't mind, because he felt fine and he was glad that she had come.

"Do you think I might have a cup of coffee?" she said. But she kissed him instead. The kitchen was quiet and sunny. Then she leaned away from him and said, "Some of that good old-fashioned coffee you're so famous for?"

"You smell good."

"It's Charlie," she breathed.

"Charlie of Harlem?"

"Perfume," she sighed.

They drank their coffee on the back porch in the sun. Swipesy lay between them and slept. Swipesy was Loney's dog. He was very old and deaf. Rhea patted his head and they were silent for several minutes. Then she looked at Loney and said. "You're so beautiful today. So doggone gorgeous."

"Thank you," said Loney.

"You're so damned lovely sometimes. Sometimes I think I would just like to take a bite of you."

"We could go inside," said Loney.

"I love your dark skin and your dark hair, your noble dark profile. Sometimes you remind me of a dark greyhound. Do you mind?"

"You want to gnaw on my arm?"

"I want to gnaw on your throat," she growled.

"Everything I have is yours."

"That's a song, show-off." She sipped her coffee. It was half milk and barely warm. "I feel so perfect today. Thank you for being so . . . in shape."

"It's my pleasure."

"And so gallant. I believe you're my Southern gentleman today."

Loney looked at her. He looked at her eyes and he wondered at them. Sometimes they were the color of turquoise and he wondered at their coldness, but in that morning light they were the warm green of alfalfa and he wondered at their depth and his own good luck.

"Let's go for a drive. I know just the place," she said.

"Not Havre." Sometimes on Saturday they drove to Havre for a matinee.

"There." And she pointed to the Little Rockies. From the porch they could just see the small range.

"Do you really want to?"

"It will do us a world of good. Let's feed old Swipesy here and then we'll go to Buttrey's and pick out some cheese and then we'll get a nice bottle of white wine. You go put your jacket on. I'll feed Swipesy. I know how. Tomato soup, right?" She stood and brushed the seat of her jeans. For just this one day she wanted it all.

6

They sat in Rhea's small station wagon in a grove of alders just out of sight of the main road. Three yellow leaves lay on the hood of the car. They had eaten the small round of Camembert cheese and drunk enough of the wine to feel lazy.

"How did those leaves get on my car?"

"They fell from that tree."

"In November?"

"They were waiting for us."

They sat and watched the dark clouds that had appeared suddenly over the east rim of the canyon. They were coming fast and widening to the south.

"Do you think it will snow?"

"Something is blowing in. I don't know."

"And what's the name of this canyon?"

"Mission."

"And what's the name of that mission back there?"

"St. Paul's? That's funny. I don't remember. I used to play basketball against them."

"And did you win?"

"They weren't very good. It's a small school."

"I love it out here. It's so peaceful. Do you think anybody ever comes here?"

"Hunters, picnickers. People gathering chokecherries."

"Let's build a cabin. We can cut down these little old trees. We'll build a log cabin and you can hunt. Just like your ancestors. You can dress me up in furs. Are there any ermines here?"

"Weasels. They turn into ermines in the winter."

"Do you ever think about your ancestors?"

"Which ones?"

"Whichever you claim. Oh, you're so lucky to have two sets of ancestors. Just think, you can be Indian one day and white the next. Whichever suits you."

The clouds had covered the sun while they were talking and the car had begun to get cold. Loney thought, It would be nice to think that, but it would be nicer to be one or the other all the time, to have only one set of ancestors. It would be nice to think that one was one or the other, Indian or white. Whichever, it would be nicer than being a half-breed.

"What suits you now, Mr. Loney?"

And Loney pulled her to him. He was grateful that Rhea didn't want him to be anything now but here. He kissed her and he held her and he felt her small breasts roll softly against his chest. In the cramped front seat he undressed her and she unbuttoned his shirt and unclasped his belt. Her cold delicate fingers stroked his chest and he didn't think about his ancestors. He moved from behind the steering wheel and she straddled him, her cheek pressed to his ear. She felt contented, even drowsy from the wine. She closed her eyes and smelled his hair oil and when she opened them she saw a deer through the rear window. It was a large deer, without antlers. It stood broadside, its head turned directly toward the car. Rhea watched it flick its right ear, then lift a hind hoof to scratch it. She almost exclaimed, but she felt drowsy and she felt Loney's hand urging her down onto his lap. She closed her eyes because she wanted to give herself to him and she closed her eyes because she was drowsy and she wanted to keep this one secret. She kissed his neck and she felt him inside her and she thought, One day I will tell him. For that moment it was the best secret ever.

7

"I never really thought about it. It was so long ago and I was just a kid. He just left. It was really that simple—here today, gone tomorrow. I think it affected Kate more because she was older. She was old enough to expect something from him. I guess he wasn't much of a father. I must have been nine or ten when he left. He went out drinking one night and didn't return for twelve years. Kate was about fifteen then and she'd been taking care of me for some time already."

"What about your mother?"

"She didn't exist. She left when I was a year old. Kate sort of remembers her. At least she says she does. She was an Indian woman from out around Hays, a Westwolf maybe. Kate thinks she went crazy sometime after she left. I didn't know her."

"Would you like a glass of wine?"

"No, I have to talk. If I have a glass of wine I'll be on my way. It happens fast with me now. I think I'd better talk. Anyway, our father left when I was nine or ten. To this day I don't know where he went, but he was gone for twelve years.

"Then one day I saw him on the street. I didn't know for a long time that I had seen him. There was something familiar about the man. I don't mean he looked familiar, but there was something about the way he moved. No, that's not it either. Just a look, I guess. The way you see somebody on the street who reminds you of the way you think you must look.

"Anyway, I didn't see this man again for two or three weeks. I thought he had been a stranger passing through. I had almost forgotten him when our paths crossed again. He was drunk and was walking down the same street, the one in front of the grade school, so I decided to follow him. We walked all over town. I think we walked every street in town, sometimes around the same block a couple of times, then back downtown, then out the other way. At first I thought he knew I was following him and he was doing this to throw me off the track, but he seemed too drunk. He was really weaving around. Once he stopped under a street light and started coughing. He almost coughed his lungs out. He was on one knee and almost choking to death and I almost ran to him. But he finally quit and took off again. So I kept following him and he finally crossed the railroad tracks and turned east on that street across from the grain elevators and walked to the end of it. There was a little green trailer out there. He opened the door, then he turned around and looked right at me, then he went inside and closed the door."

"Do you think he recognized you?"

"I don't know. Twelve years had passed. No, I mean yes—yes, I think he recognized me. But I don't think he was sure. So much time, I wasn't sure. . . ."

"What happened then?"

"I remember just standing there for a long time looking at the trailer. I think I was trying to find an excuse to go up there and knock on the door. I don't remember. I do remember walking away, mixed up, thinking, I'll never know. Then I got a bright idea. I ran downtown and started checking the bars. I went to the Serviceman's first. Sylvester Chase was tending bar. I described this man to him and he knew of him but he didn't know his name. Same thing at Beanie's. Finally I ended up at Kennedy's and Kenny Hart was behind the bar. When I started to describe the man he cut me short and said, 'Sure. That's Ike. That's your old man.' "

"You must have been stunned."

"That was fourteen years ago but I remember it as though it happened this afternoon. I remember sitting down and Kenny pouring me a shot of something. I remember looking into it for a long time. Then I asked Kenny what my father was doing back in town and he said, 'This is his home, ain't it?'

"Fourteen years. We haven't talked in all that time. I was waiting for him to make the first move. I wanted him to think he had the drop on me, that I still didn't know, but I guess he didn't think it was worth it."

"This is Chablis. It's very dry. You might not like it."

"Kate talked to him once, three years ago, the last time she was out here. They had a real row. She wanted him to admit that he was our father and that he had abandoned us. She wanted him to admit that. She's funny that way, the way she wants things to be clear.

"But he wouldn't admit anything. He just quit talking. I think he holds our mother against us. We must remind him of her. I think she must have run out on him. That's how come he won't recognize us. And you know the worst of it? I don't even know what she looks like, or even if she's still alive."

"Do you hold it against her—I mean the fact that she wasn't a mother?"

"No. She just wasn't, that's all."

"And your father?"

Loney shrugged.

8

Jim Loney didn't know how long he had been asleep, but when he awoke it was close to 4 A.M. Outside, the wind swirled and blew snow like grains of sand against the kitchen window. He looked down at his dog and his dog was looking up at him.

"How you doing, old man?"

Swipesy twisted his head.

"You don't even hear me, but I think you understand everything about life. And you know that you're a good old boy, don't you? Yes, you're a good old dog. You live clean and you never abuse yourself. You're an example to me, Swipesy. I just wish I was as smart as you. I used to be. I was as smart as anybody."

Swipesy sat up and pushed his nose against Loney's knee.

"That was before I realized I didn't know anything. Not one damn thing that was worth knowing. Do you understand that? Do I understand that?" Loney allowed himself a rueful smile that had nothing to do with the dog.

He petted Swipesy until the dog slumped back to the floor. Then the lamp on the table flickered and went out. Loney sat for a moment and listened to the wind. From the dark room he could see the sheet of snow blowing through the street lamp beside the Catholic church.

He stood and walked the five feet to the refrigerator. He felt around on top of it until he found the candle. It was a blocky red candle with a plastic wreath around its base. He couldn't remember where it had come from. He hadn't celebrated Christmas since he had lived with an aunt for two years many years ago. He remembered going to midnight mass with her, then eating some kind of pudding. He tried, as always, to remember how old he had been, but as always, it didn't come to him. He recalled the flavor of that pudding and it tasted like butterscotch, but he knew it wasn't. That aunt had died. Her name was Sandra, or Susan, or something that started with an S. Sometimes he liked to think that if she hadn't died, he would have lived with her forever. She liked midnight mass and she liked many men in those two years. But he remembered most that she liked him.

He lit the candle and picked up his sister's letter. In the yellow light he read, and it was full of the usual things—her job, her social life, the men who turned out to be drips or lechers, a guided tour of the places she had been to, and finally the offer to pay his way to Washington, D.C., and to get him a job. Loney had to smile because each of her letters for the past three or four years had contained this offer. It was an offer made in earnest, but Loney could not conceive of a life in the East. She would have better luck trying to convince a zebra to live in Washington. And so he read the three pages with a kind of guilty amusement until he reached the last paragraph, which was written in a hasty scrawl with a different-colored ink, green:

> Since you do not choose to answer my letters and because I consider you my God-given burden in life, I have decided to

> take the week off at the end of this month and fly out. I would like to make it Thanksgiving, but I will be in Arizona at a meeting, *after which* I will fly to Great Falls, then to Havre. I will let you know when you can pick me up. Is your car running? Please be healthy. And *please* don't tell Dad I'm coming. It would only lead to difficulties unimaginable.

And it was signed, "Affectionately, Kate."

Loney lit a cigarette from the candle and found his hand trembling. It was not a new thing; lately it happened quite often, and he didn't know if it was a physical thing or if it was just because of the cigarettes and wine and lack of sleep. He made fists until the knuckles turned white, but still his hands shook. And again, as he had that night after the football game, he saw things strangely, yet clearly. The candle, the wine bottle, the letter before him, all burned clearly in his eyes and they had no reality in his mind. It was as though there were no connection between his eyes and his brain. And he saw the smoke ring go out away from his face and he saw the bird in flight. Like the trembling, the bird was not new. It came every night now. It was a large bird and dark. It was neither graceful nor clumsy, and yet it was both. Sometimes the powerful wings beat the air with the monotony of grace; at other times, it seemed that the strokes were out of tune, as though the bird had lost its one natural ability and was destined to eventually lose the air. But it stayed up and Loney watched it until it reached into the darkness beyond the small candlelight.

Loney picked up his glass. It was half full of wine. "Here's to the bird, my bird," he said. His mouth was dry and the wine did not taste good. He was restless. He had been thinking of his life for a month. He had tried to think of all the little things that added up to a man sitting at a table drinking wine. But he couldn't connect the different parts of his life, or the various people who had entered and left it. Sometimes he felt like an amnesiac searching for the one event, the one person or moment, that would bring everything back and he would see the order in his life. But without the amnesiac's clean slate, all the people and events were as hopelessly tangled as a bird's nest in his mind, and so for almost a month he had been sitting at his table, drinking wine, and saying to himself, "Okay, from this very moment I will start back—I will think of yesterday, last week, last year, until all my years are accounted for. Then I will look ahead and know where I'm going." But the days piled up faster than the years receded and he grew restless and despondent. But he would not concede that his life had added up to nothing more than the simple reality of a man sitting and drinking in a small house in the world.

And so he drank to the bird which came every night and he tried to attach some significance to it, but the bird remained as real and as elusive as the wine and cigarettes and his own life.

Swipesy whimpered in his sleep and Loney came back. He picked up the letter and turned again to the last paragraph. *The end of this month.* November. But he had no idea what the date was. He tried to think of something that had happened that would help, but the only thing he could think of was snow. And Rhea. He hadn't seen her for several days, since the trip out to Mission Canyon. He would see her soon. He would clean up again and he would see her. Like a first anniversary. They had met almost a year ago at a basketball game. She had been selling tickets and she had been curt with him because she did not consider it part of her duties as an English teacher to sell tickets to a basketball game. But then she apologized and they talked for a few minutes. Loney had flattered himself that she recognized him from his picture in the trophy case at school. He had been on the team that won Harlem's only state championship. In the picture he was kneeling beside Myron Pretty Weasel, who was holding the basketball that read STATE B CHAMPS 1958. But she hadn't seen the picture; in fact, she hadn't even noticed the trophy case.

But a couple of weeks later she did recognize him in the grocery store. On an impulse she invited him home for dinner and she slept with him that night. They were both surprised. Loney couldn't believe that such a lovely classy woman would want him and Rhea couldn't believe it either. She had come north to escape entanglements. She told him this later. She admitted that at first he represented only warmth and sex. He had settled for that, but now, a year later, they were lovers and he was blowing it. And he didn't know why.

November. *This month.* He picked up the envelope and read the postmark: November 12. It must be the fifteenth or sixteenth. The candle flickered in a sudden draft of wind that rattled the back door. Kate would be here in two weeks. Loney poured himself a glass of wine.

9

He didn't know when they came, only that his father came first. He had been staring at the candle when he heard the scratching on the windowpane and looked up to see his father grinning through his whiskers. His pale face seemed even whiter as the snow whirled about him. He said, "Why are you weeping?"

And Loney looked at him and the hard snow pelted the glass between them.

"Come on, I'm your father," said his father.

"But I'm not weeping," Loney said. "I'm laughing. I'm drinking wine and laughing. This is a celebration."

"You are weeping."

"But don't you see how funny it is?"

"Nothing in this world is funny."

Then Loney was standing beside his father, looking in at the weeping man. "He is weeping," Loney said.

"Of course," said his father. "Didn't I just say that? Things are not well with him."

"He is weeping for nothing, though. That's the way with him."

"No," said the father. "He is weeping for something. I ought to know."

And the son said, "He is crying for himself. He has no family."

And the father said, "That's impossible. He's crying for me. I'm his family and he pities me."

"But you have everything! You have no children. You're the best father imaginable. . . ."

"That will be enough! Enough to know he pities me, that's good enough for me."

And a third voice, muffled and far away, said, "You think too much of yourselves. Anybody can tell he misses me already; he uses his tears to good purpose." In the darkness of the room, beyond the arc of the candle, beyond the weeping man, stood a small figure with blond hair, with white teeth and green eyes.

"But I'm laughing." The man lifted his head and the tears streamed down his cheeks. "I have no one. It's a celebration."

And Loney stood beside his father and said, "He weeps, all right."

"Then why?" His father sounded indignant.

"And why?" Rhea sounded impatient.

Loney rubbed his chin, lost in thought. He lit a cigarette, lost in thought. Then he took a sip of wine and the wine exploded. "I've got it! He weeps for us, for all of us!"

"How so?"

"Because he can't have us."

"How so?"
"Because we are lost to him."
"No!" exclaimed a fourth voice. "Can't you see the man wants only to be left alone, to think?"
"But he is alone," sniffed Rhea.
"Alone as that bird he would believe in," sniffed the father.
And the man sobbed, "No, no, I am not alone, but I weep for no one. I weep only to myself. It's a simplicity I have learned."
"See?" said the son. "He weeps only to himself. He's a selfish one."
And Rhea and the father agreed.
"He's not selfish at all," said the fourth voice. "He just . . . hurts."
"Don't we all!" exclaimed the father. "Don't I hurt most of all? This man is a prince next to me."
"A prince!" exclaimed the son.
"And you brought it all on yourself," said the fourth voice. "If you hurt, you deserve it."
And Loney recognized the fourth voice.
"That's the way you talk to your father," said the father.
"You deserve it and more," said the sister. "You deserve to live."
"But why? What have you got against me?"
"Ask him." And Kate pointed to Loney.
But the father didn't ask him. He simply looked at Loney and Loney saw the snow sticking to his whiskers. Then that pale grin came back and he pressed something long and heavy into Loney's arms. "You might need this," he said, "where you're going." Loney looked down and saw the dark blue barrel and the burnished wood of a shotgun. Then he looked up and his father was gone. Rhea was gone. His sister was gone. He looked into the window and the man who had been crying or laughing only seconds before was now wearily pinching out the candle with his fingers.

10

Rhea sat at the table in the dining nook and reread the letter. There was something so clean about it. For one thing, it had been typed and there was not an error in it. For another, the language was crisp, businesslike, and pointed toward a particular conclusion. And it was this conclusion that Rhea marveled at. It was the only one and yet it was the one that Rhea had not expected: Kate wanted to take Loney back to Washington with her.

Rhea fingered the sectioned ivory choker at her neck. She wore it over a black turtleneck. She wasn't wearing makeup and she imagined that her face looked as stark as the ivory.

Her first reaction to the letter was, Why on earth would she want to do that? But even as she read the letter she knew exactly why. And she knew that she had instigated it. She had written Kate first. She had gotten Kate's address from one of the letters on Loney's table. And she had written Kate that she was becoming concerned about his drinking, and even more about his desire to isolate himself. Rhea had written that she was the only one he saw anymore. He had been this way for almost two months. He hardly ever left his house except when he needed things, mostly wine and cigarettes. She concluded that he seemed to be suffering (and she remembered her own phrase) "a crisis of spirit." But, she thought, it was exactly that, a crisis, something to be gotten over. After all, one doesn't simply lapse into malaise, never to rise again. But she had worried in the letter about how much good she could do him; he seemed to be going away from her too.

And so she had received this answer, this conclusion that Kate had come to several years before. And now Kate wanted her help. She wanted Rhea to prepare him for the big move.

And that was what she marveled at. That Kate knew she would be taking her brother away from Rhea. There was an assumption in the letter that it would be to Rhea's own interest to help her. And a further assumption that Kate considered her brother incapable of steering his own course.

Rhea stood and looked out the window above the table. And she felt that familiar anger every time she had to stand to see what the world was doing. The man must have thought he was building a house for giants, she thought. She watched the snow skitter low over the yard. The pale sunlight struck the snow and it reminded her of airplane trips above the clouds.

And she discovered it, the thought that had been in the back of her mind all morning: Kate was stealing her thunder, and that's what irritated her most about the letter. She almost smiled in recognition. *She* had been thinking of getting Loney away from Harlem. But she did not have a plan of attack. The possibility of it had not really occurred to her. It had all been fantasy.

Rhea let her breath out and it fogged a small oval on the window. She felt that emptiness that came whenever she tried to imagine a life with Loney. Sometimes she imagined taking him home to Dallas. She imagined him meeting her father and mother, her friends, her grandmother. She couldn't think of anything more disastrous.

So her most common fantasy involved starting fresh in a place where neither of them had been. Lately that fantasy place was Seattle. She liked the idea of lush greenery, of mountains and salt water. Her friend Colleen was from Seattle and Colleen had painted a picture of heaven on earth. It did sound like the perfect place, and not far. They could be there in two days. Maybe he wouldn't feel so *displaced.*

Rhea walked over to the stove and turned the burner on beneath the teakettle, and she thought of her own letter to Kate. She must have sounded desperate. She had written it a couple of days before she and Loney had driven out to the

Little Rockies. But the trip, and the fact that Loney had put his house in order, made Rhea think that he had reached, and passed, that crisis point and that he was on his way to some purpose. And it was up to her to give him that purpose.

Oh, God, I'm just like some high school girl planning to trap an unsuspecting boy, she thought. She had always hated that.

11

The sun was a high disk in a white sky. Beneath it, everything—the trees, the butte to the south, the Little Rockies—looked steel gray. The houses of Harlem were bundled up and the snow squealed underfoot. The low brick buildings of downtown reflected nothing of the sun and nothing stirred. The only color in the street belonged to a turquoise and white Ford parked in front of the laundromat. Its windows were frosted over.

Loney pulled his parka tighter around his neck. The zipper was broken and only the drawstring around his middle held it together. He walked with his head down against a gusting wind out of the north which sent the loose snow scurrying low in the street. He walked past the drugstore, the liquor store and the bank. Then he crossed the old highway and the railroad tracks. He turned east on the street that paralleled the tracks and walked to the end of it.

He stood in the road a hundred feet from the little green trailer. A narrow path up to the door had been drifted over. The wind blew harder at this end of town and only a deeper blue in the color of the snow betrayed the path.

"Hey!" he yelled. "Hey!"

He stood very still and waited. And nothing happened. No one came to the door, the curtain at the window didn't move. He made a snowball and threw it in the direction of the trailer, but it landed way short and exploded against a broken wagon wheel that was once part of a fence. "I know you're in there!" He made another snowball, but this one disintegrated as soon as it left his hand, the wind blowing the cold powder back into his face. "Come out here," he sputtered.

He stood on the edge of town, and the white fields behind the trailer were broken only by fencelines and stacks of bales. Beyond the fields, the prairies lifted and rolled toward Canada.

"I need to talk to you!" But nothing. There was no sound except for the quickening wind. He put his hood up and looked around for something else to throw, but the snow had covered everything. He clenched his parka tight around his middle and the wind entered his body and he felt his eyes go wet.

He tried to look at the trailer, but it blurred into the white fields, the prairies and the yellow-gray sky. It was Sunday.

"You bastard!" he cried.

12

"What in the world . . ."

"I was walking around."

"You must be freezing. Come in. How about this wind? Isn't it awful, how it just came up?" She grabbed Loney's hand and pulled him through the doorway. "I can't get over it!"

"I think I might have something to do with it," he said.

"Well, of course! You have everything to do with it."

Rhea sat him down on the rug in front of the fireplace. A couple of small cottonwood logs were smoking. "Sit here by the fire. Maybe you can do something with it. I'll get you something hot."

Loney watched her walk away, her bare feet small and white against the beige rug. He glanced around the room. He hadn't been to Rhea's house very often and it seemed new to him each time. He looked wistfully at the furniture. It was all leather and wood and graceful. He had never seen that kind before. Real paintings hung on the walls, but they were the kind he couldn't be sure about.

"I hope you like this tea," she called. "It's very Oriental."

In spite of her gaiety, he sensed that certain formality he had come to associate with Southern hospitality. It perplexed him. When they were in his house they argued, joked, made love—sometimes they wrestled, and once they ate canned stew off the same plate. But here, in her apartment, they were almost formal. He knew he was not a good guest. He never felt comfortable in other people's homes. He hadn't been in many and he touched as few things as possible.

He stood and walked to the sliding doors in the south wall. A plant as tall as he glistened in the dying light. He examined one of the broad shiny leaves; then he looked at the glass but he didn't look beyond it.

"Have you got that fire fixed?" she said as she entered the room. "Oh, you!" But she was happy. She made a face and he saw her white teeth. He would remember them long after she was gone. And he felt bad for having thought such a thought. "Well, come here. We'll try it together."

She set his cup of tea on a table near the fireplace. He watched the steam roll away and he thought briefly of the aunt he had lived with. She and Loney always had cocoa together in the evening. She gave him all he wanted and he always wanted more. He hadn't had cocoa since.

"Oh, look!" Rhea said. She had put another log on and the fire flared up. "I guess it just takes an expert, Mr. Loney."

He stood beside her and they were both still, watching the fire grow, watching as their thoughts grew. In the quiet of that darkening room, Loney looked into the fire and he saw his dark bird. Its long dark wings moved slowly up and down just above the flames. Tonight it was graceful and he was grateful. And he wanted her to see it too, but he knew she didn't. She had her own thoughts. And Loney felt like a beggar standing beside her because her mind was rich, and he envied her.

"You must be very gentle," she said. "This night, right now, you must be a lamb." And she looked up at him. "Won't you?"

He watched the bird getting smaller and he felt bad. He had wanted to share this moment.

13

As Rhea watched him sleep she thought two things: She thought that Loney was a funny name and she thought she had never watched him sleep. And she thought that somehow the two thoughts were connected, that people who were truly alone slept very little and that to watch one sleep was like watching a hummingbird at rest. Even in those early days when they were new to each other and happy, she had never seen him sleep. But then she had interpreted this as a mark of strength, of consideration, a funny manly think to do. She remembered so many times falling asleep in his arms and waking up in his arms, and he was always awake. She had loved this about him and she did not consider it a foolish thing. She was used to men doing foolish things for her; sometimes she made them do foolish things, like the time she had made one of them swim out to her even though she knew he couldn't swim, and he did almost drown. But that was years ago, that was Galveston, and she had been silly then. She shuddered to think how silly, but more, to think that it had been only two and a half years ago, the summer before she came up to this place, and the man was the man she was engaged to. He was a lawyer, just out of law school, and he loved opera. And he loved her. He once introduced her to Beverly Sills and he told her later that it had been the supreme moment in his life, introducing the two women he loved. She had been impressed with his family's connections but not overwhelmed. Her own family, while not being that close to Beverly Sills, had gone to all the fund-raising dinners for the symphony and the theater, and had contributed loads of money to the Southern Methodist football team, and her father had met Don Meredith. Rhea had only a vague notion of Don Meredith's importance, but her father thought a few minutes with him was worth a lifetime of making cardboard boxes and pontoons for houseboats and acquiring land. In fact, her father was a millionaire, and because he was a millionaire, he got to meet Don Meredith, just as other millionaires got to meet Beverly Sills. Dallas was full of millionaires dying to meet somebody famous. More often than not they met each other and decried Houston, where millionaires met astronauts. And Presidents came to speak and meet astronauts. And millionaires.

Now, a million miles away from Houston, and Dallas, and Galveston, watching Loney sleep, Rhea thought a third thing: How strange. How very strange. To run away from things. To run away from her family. And a man she was engaged to. It wasn't like her to have the courage. To run away. To end up teaching school. Here. In this place away from anywhere. And most of all, to end up sleeping with this man who doesn't sleep but is asleep now. A dark hummingbird at rest.

She moved away from him and stood and walked to the sliding door. The fire had gone out and the room was dark. She touched a slick leaf of the plant and looked up at the three-quarter moon. "Loney, Loney," she said, and she felt foolish.

She tiptoed into the kitchen. The small light over the stove cast more shadow than light, but she found the bottle of wine in the cupboard under the sink. She poured a stemmed glass half full and carried it into the living room. She found Loney's parka draped over the back of a chair and searched its pockets until she came up with his cigarettes. Such a tattered coat. He hadn't smoked all night. She lit a cigarette with the large crystal lighter that her mother had given her. And it struck her as an odd sort of gift. And it struck her odd that she had replaced it in its precise position on the coffee table. Southern womanhood, she thought, and that seemed most absurd of all.

She sat on one of the low leather chairs and tucked her feet up under her. She wondered how she looked, drink in one hand, cigarette in the other. At the moment, even in her wondering, she didn't care. She was at home. And not at home. But at least, she thought, I am something wherever I am. In my best moments.

And so she drank and smoked and looked out at the stark houses draped in stark moonlight. Nothing moved in the street. Around midnight Loney stirred and said, "I'm small," and she wondered if he had been awake all along, or if he ever truly slept, but he said nothing else, and she lost track of time.

Once during the early morning she awoke to a dog's bark and she could feel its frosty breath. And another time, near dawn, she heard a solemn voice, out of the crowd of her own thoughts, say, "Rhea, you're the only friend I've got in the whole world."

"I know," she heard her own clean voice say, "and it frightens me." And she watched dawn and thought about Seattle.

14

Loney dreamed long and he dreamed in detail. Among his other dreams he dreamed of a church and it was the Catholic church down in the valley east of the agency. It sat high on a knoll beside the highway and it was pink, with four high windows on each side. Above the rooftree a metal cross glinted in the winter sun. He was alone, standing on the step and feeling small, looking up at the padlocked plank doors. He examined the heavy metal straps that held the doors in place. Then he moved up and ran his fingers over the stucco beside the door. He seemed to be searching for something, but it was not inside the church. He started down the steps and when he reached the hard earth of the knoll he heard a sound that could have been the wind had there been any. The sound was far away and regular, as though a tree limb were rubbing against the roof. It came from behind the church and so he walked that way. He stopped at the corner and looked to where the knoll rounded off to descend into the valley and he saw a woman. He saw her back and she was wearing a shawl up over her head. He walked toward her. Her shoulders were slumped and her head was down. He walked between the graves, and the earth was hard and bare. He stopped behind her. And she was weeping. Rather, she was wailing, the way Indian women wail for their lost ones. He didn't disturb her. He watched her until she became aware of his presence. When she turned he saw that she was young, and this surprised him.

Her face was beautiful and it was made up and her lipstick was a dark red. There was something old-fashioned about her makeup. And Loney noticed that her dress was old-fashioned, the way women dressed in pictures thirty years ago. She dropped her shawl to her shoulders and smiled at him. There were no tears in her eyes. He had the feeling that she was going to ask him to buy her a drink, but she said, "My son is gone."

He looked down at the grave and said, "He's here."

The woman turned and made a sweeping gesture out across the dark prairies behind them. "My son is out there," she said.

Loney looked out across the prairies to the Little Rockies. They were high and blue beneath the snowy peaks. Then he said to the woman, "Who are you?"

"A mother," she said. "A mother who is no longer a mother."

"But you're more than that. You're young and beautiful. . . ."

"And I have no son." The woman looked down at the grave. "He's not here."

"Then you are not a mother."

"He is somewhere—out there. But I will never find him because he will not allow himself to be found."

Loney stared at her face. Beneath the makeup her skin was dark and smooth. It was as though she wore the makeup as a mask, as though she had disguised herself, but for a purpose that eluded him. He found himself attracted to that face beneath the makeup, but he couldn't see it clearly enough to know why. It was not a face that he was familiar with, and yet it was a face he had seen before.

The woman put the shawl back up over her head and started walking toward the church. Loney glanced down at the grave, then after her. "I'll help you find him," he called. And he saw the shawl tighten across her shoulders. As she turned the corner of the building, he called, "What does he look like?" And she disappeared.

15

Loney tried to drink his beer, but the drunk woman hit his arm again.

"Do you believe in astrology?"

"I don't read the newspaper."

"That's a dumbass answer if I ever heard one. I don't even know why I talk to you."

Don't, then, he thought. But he said, "I'm not unintelligent."

"Well, la-di-da. The man can rub a couple of words together." She turned with great wonder to the man next to her and laughed. But he was not having any of it. He appeared to be sulking about something. He was an older man and he was wearing a denim shirt and Levi's.

"I'm not unintelligent," Loney said.

"Okay, Mr. Brighteyes, maybe you'd know your own sign if you were that smart."

"I have no reason to be smart anymore."

"What? What? No reason? Since when does a body need a reason?" She looked at Loney as though she might strike him if he gave the wrong answer. She was a white woman but she looked as though she might have some Indian blood. Her eyes were dark brown and she combed her long brown hair the way some Indian women do. "Oh, I get it—what you see is what you get." She again turned to the sulking man. "What you see is what you get. Isn't that right, Clancy?"

"Go fuck a dog," said Clancy.

"Pretty good," said the woman. She leaned toward Loney and said in a loud voice, "See, he doesn't even get what he sees. This old boy don't get nothin' anymore. You know why?"

"I don't want to know."

"Cuz he has a teensy little problem. I believe they call it i-m-p-o-t-e-n-c-e."

"Go fuck yourself," said Clancy.

"Be the best piece I've had in a long time." She touched Loney's hand. "You know what else? On top of that he has sugar diabetes."

"Pay no attention to her," said Clancy. He hadn't looked at Loney once. "She's a shit."

"Poopface," said the woman, but she settled back on her stool, satisfied that she had made Clancy's life miserable.

Loney got up and walked back to the bathroom. He had been sitting beside the woman for over two hours and it had been the same rough talk and he wondered what made some women so hard, especially bar women. When they reached a certain age they just got hard. Loney thought of the women he had seen who could sit on a stool all night without getting drunk, or at least visibly drunk, but when you looked into their eyes you could see the hardness, as cold and hard as the January earth. He wondered what they were like at home, if they sent kids off to school in the morning, if they made cakes, if they made love, if they loved anyone. He wondered if the woman loved Clancy or if Clancy loved her. It seemed an odd relationship, but he had seen it before, the loud-mouthed woman, the sullen man. It was only different because Clancy seemed to have twenty or thirty years on her. But Loney had seen that too. And he didn't like the way the woman treated the old man. He wondered why they were together, why people like that stayed with each other.

What about himself and Rhea? Every time he thought of her, he thought how badly he had been treating her the past few weeks, how he had been shutting her out, and how she had been willing to accept him when he needed her. He washed his hands and dried them on his pants. He closed his eyes and said, "I'm the one, not that woman out there, who's a shit." And he didn't know how to change it. The more he thought about himself, his life, his family, the more he shut her out. Until he needed her. And yet he could admit to himself that he did need her. He loved being with her. He loved the weekend before, the trip out to the Little Rockies, being in her house, sleeping with her on the rug. He loved those times, but always, afterward, he feared them. He didn't know how their lives could end up happily, how his life would end up. He knew he couldn't be just himself with her forever, because he was nothing. She came from better things and she would need him to be better. And he couldn't think of a way in the world to be good enough. And that's what frightened him.

He knew he shouldn't be thinking this way now because he was tired, and drunk, although not as drunk as he had been the week before. He had sat that week at his kitchen table, drinking and smoking and trying to think. For the first time in his life he had tried to understand a dream, the dream of the young woman in the graveyard behind the church. He had tried day after day to recognize her and to remember if he knew anybody buried in that cemetery. He tried to figure out why she was dressed that way and why she wore the makeup and why she insisted that her son was gone and why she thought he would not allow himself to be found. But most of all he wondered whether, if he had followed her when she turned the corner of the church, the dream would have ended. But in his lucid moments he knew he didn't have a choice, that when she disappeared she was gone to him for good.

He tried not to think of it now. He should go home, he was tired, but it was early yet. It couldn't be much after nine. He had come downtown at dusk, just after the shoppers had gone home. He had bathed and shaved and now he was out for drinks. It sounded innocent and natural to him when he thought of it like that. Like ten years ago, when he went out to find women.

He walked back up to the bar and he saw the pay phone on the wall beside the pool table. Four young Indians were shooting a game and joking around. He recognized one of them, a skinny kid who had been a basketball star a couple of years ago. His face had gotten a little heavy.

Loney edged around the table. He looked up Rhea's number in the phone book. He didn't have a phone and he had never called her. It surprised him to be dialing it and he felt a little tense. Then he heard the click of the phone being picked up and he heard her voice.

"This is Jim," he said.

A pause, then her voice said, "Jim?"

"I called you up. Loney."

"Oh! Oh! Jim! Oh, Jim. You gave me such a start. I almost had kittens."

"I thought I would call you up."

"Oh, lord!" And then her voice changed. "Are you all right?"

"Yes. I was just worried. I haven't heard from you. . . ."

And she was silent again. In the background Loney heard music and loud indistinct voices. Finally she said, "I'm having a party."

Loney watched the basketball star line up a shot. He drilled it and the cue ball jumped off the table.

Then he heard her voice. "An impromptu party. One of those kind that happen when the weather changes."

"Thanksgiving party?"

"I suppose. I hadn't thought of it, but that sounds reasonable."

"I just called you," Loney said and he realized his mistake.

"Will you come over? Please?"

The basketball star had chased down the cue ball. He had a silly grin on his face, as though he didn't know his own strength.

"It's important," she said. "Are you drunk?"

"No," he lied.

"Will you come over?"

"Yes," he said.

One of the boys yelled and held his cue stick high above

his head. He had sunk the eight ball. The star put a quarter in the pool table, pushed a lever, and the balls came rolling out, clicking and clattering along a track. He wasn't grinning anymore.

Loney hung up the phone and walked toward the bar. Kenny Hart was waiting down at the dark end. He was smiling. He looked fat and puffy, but beneath the spectacles, his nose was crooked. "Hey, c'mere." He motioned with his finger. "Hey—" He leaned over the bar. "You know why a North Dakotan carries a turd in his wallet?"

Loney looked at his wavy gray hair.

"Give up?" The smile stayed but he looked tense. "No, c'mere." He gripped Loney's wrist. "I'm serious. For ID. He carries a turd around for ID. Are you all right? I've been watching you." His hand felt soft, but Loney couldn't move his wrist. "Listen—you stay away from those people. That old man, he's a friend of mine. That woman, she ain't worth a shit. Wait a minute." He was talking more rapidly. "See, he can't cut it anymore. He used to be worth more than you and me put together. He was a pretty fair hand once, he was the best, up until his wife left him. Just like your old man. Now I want you to stay away from them. That's all. She gets to showing off at his expense. You know? She's nothing but a bitch and you can't get around that. But we'll just leave them alone. Why don't you sit down here? Let me buy you one."

Loney tried to think about this. He was very tired.

"How about another, pal?"

"I want a bottle to go."

"F-I?"

Loney thought of Rhea and her good wine. "What else you got?"

"Thunderbird and Mogen David."

"Mogen David," said Loney.

"That's the idea. You'll never regret it, partner."

Kenny Hart came back with a bottle in a sack. "On the

house. Listen, why the hell do you stay away so long?"

Loney walked by the old man and the woman. She had her arm around him. She was singing "Frosty the Snowman" to the bar.

16

Rhea met him at the door and took the bottle from him. "I'll get you a drink. Where in the world were you calling from?"

"Kennedy's."

She took his parka and threw it over a table in the hallway. "Come into the kitchen."

Loney glanced into the living room and wished he hadn't come. All of the guests were white and respectable. The men wore sweaters or sports coats, or both, and the women wore dresses or sweaters and slacks. They were all clean and they stood in groups and gestured with their drinks. Loney recognized a couple of them. One was the basketball coach, a big slick-haired man with thin lips and sad brown eyes. He had been the coach for three years and he never seemed to get upset, just sadder as his teams continued to break his heart.

And Loney recognized Rhea's friend Colleen, a slender woman with wire-rimmed glasses and black hair parted in the middle. She was Rhea's closest friend because she, too, was an outsider, from the West Coast. Before he met Rhea, he and Colleen had screwed outside the rodeo grounds at the Phillips County Fair. They didn't know each other and they were drunk and it didn't count for anything, so they both forgot about it. Later, in a bar in Dodson, she told him that he was no good and she didn't like him. Now she looked up.

In the kitchen Rhea said, "What's your pleasure, partner?"

"I should leave."

"No, please." She poured some bourbon into a glass. "You're not drunk?" she said.

"I don't know. I don't think I should be here."

"It's important," she said. Above the music she said, "It's important," but she didn't know what she was going to tell him. She thought of Kate's letter and her own desires and she became nervous.

Then the basketball coach was standing in the doorway. "Jim Loney," he said and shook his head.

"I gather you two know each other," said Rhea.

The coach shook his head and turned and drifted away.

Loney wanted to tell Rhea that no one knew him anymore, not out of self-pity but to set her mind at ease. In the past several years he had become something of a nonperson, as one only can in a small town, a small town in Montana.

Rhea dropped two ice cubes in the glass of bourbon, then handed it to him. "Will you come meet some of the guests?"

Loney suddenly felt exhausted. He had been temporarily revived by the walk over in the cold air. But the warmth of the room, the voices and the music, his own tenseness, made him feel faint.

A young couple came into the kitchen to refill their drinks and Rhea introduced them to Loney. The woman said, "How do you do?" but the man pushed past on his way to the bar. The woman raised her hands and made a face; then she followed her husband.

"Come with me," Rhea said. And she led him down the hall to her bedroom. A small light burned on a table near the bed. The bed was piled high with coats.

Rhea looked at the coats and she said something Loney couldn't hear. She led him to a room across the hall and closed the door behind them. It was her study. She took Loney's drink and set it on a table beside a day bed. Then she pushed him down and sat next to him.

"You look awful," she said.

But the room was cooler and Loney felt better. Rhea massaged the back of his neck and her fingers were cool and light. Loney sighed. He felt almost giddy with exhaustion and her touch.

"I'm sorry," he said.

"I shouldn't have made you come."

"It doesn't matter—here or there. I should have stayed home." He tried to laugh and it sounded foreign to him.

"You're shivering." And she left the room.

Loney saw his drink on the table and it looked golden and cold, but he didn't have the energy to reach for it. Then he heard a voice.

"Well, Mr. Loney, people are just dying to meet you-all."

He turned his head and it seemed to take a long time.

Colleen leaned against the doorframe, holding a cigarette close to her mouth. Behind the round panes of her glasses, her eyes were dark and drunk.

He looked at her and he couldn't think of anything to say. Then Rhea was squeezing by her. She had a sweater. It was dark green with red deer marching across the chest. "Do you remember this? I gave it to you last Christmas. You never took it home."

Loney didn't remember the sweater and for an instant he thought she had taken it off one of her guests. He tried to remember last Christmas.

Rhea stood over him and pulled the sweater down over his head. His eyes fixed on her face. She pulled his shirt collar up and patted it. Then she ran her fingers through his hair, pushing it back into some kind of order. "Isn't he an angel?" she said, but without conviction.

"Are you just going to keep him to yourself, Miss Davis? There are all kinds of people out here just waiting for their chance."

"Let them wait."

"They want to see who it is you've been keeping company with, honey."

"Don't," Rhea warned.

"You might say Mr. Loney here is the mystery guest."

"Please don't. Please go away."

Colleen ignored her. "It's cold out there, Mr. Loney."

Loney tried to stand, but Rhea put her hands on his shoulders. She turned to Colleen: "Why are you doing this?"

"I'm just trying to warm Mr. Loney up to the atmosphere, sweetie."

"Get out," Rhea snapped.

For an instant Colleen looked nonplused. Then she said, "I'd have thought better of you." Then she was gone.

Rhea knelt before Loney and looked into his eyes. They were flat and out of focus. Poor man, she thought. My poor man.

She sat back on her heels. She absently traced a star on his knee with her fingernail. Then she said, "Can you hear me?"

His eyes came back.

"Would you like to lie down? I'll turn off the light."

"Yes."

And she lay down beside him. She heard the throbbing music and the dark and sudden laughter, but it was far away. "Do you remember I said I had something important to tell you?"

It was dark and she wondered exactly how she was going to phrase it. In fact, up until a few minutes ago she hadn't known what she was going to tell him. She had been vacillating between presenting his sister's argument and presenting her own, which was quite simple. And so she said, "I've been thinking lately of leaving Harlem for good. I don't think there's anything here for me. I miss certain things—my family, certain friends, city life, the South. I miss them but I don't feel compelled to return to them. I do feel that I have to leave here. And so I'm in something of a dilemma." She lay on her back and looked up at the ceiling. Their bodies touched on the narrow bed, yet they did not touch each other. Rhea gathered her breath. "I've been thinking of going out to Seattle. I don't really know what's out there but trees and rain. I've heard that it's very beautiful and there will be things to do. I don't even know what I want to do yet, but there are options there, maybe even a kind of salvation." She turned toward him, raising herself to her elbow. Her eyes had become accustomed to the dark and she looked at his eyes and they were open. "Do you think—would you like Seattle?"

Loney tried to remember Seattle. He had been sent to Fort Lewis for basic training sixteen years ago and he had gotten up to Seattle a couple of times. He remembered the bus rides up and the bus rides back and he remembered the trees and hills and the Boeing airfield. He had seen his first jet airplane on one of those trips. And he saw in his mind the suddenness beyond the last hill of the Seattle skyline, the buildings and the bay and the ships. The bus had let him and the other soldiers off downtown and he spent much of his time wandering around, walking into the pinball arcades, the movie houses, the cafés on First Avenue. He didn't drink then, so he didn't have any use for the bars. Instead, he usually found himself down on the waterfront, looking at ships, poking through the import shops, and watching ferries motor back and forth to a land on the other side of the bay. One clear day, he saw the Olympic range and he wanted to go there, but the thought of riding a ferry scared him.

He remembered more of Seattle than he would have thought and he remembered that he liked it and it scared him. He was older now.

"It's surrounded by mountains," he heard himself saying, "but they're a long way off. Some days you can't see them, but other days they're very close and you can see the snow. Sometimes the clouds hang down at the base of them and all you see are the peaks. They have ferryboats there and you can take your car and drive to those mountains. Or you can stay down at the waterfront and browse in the shops. They have everything from all over the world. I sent Kate some salt and pepper shakers that were bears and made of ivory and they were carved by Eskimos. I was in the army then."

Loney thought for a moment. He remembered the gray days, the rain and the chilly wind off the sound, and the couples that walked along the breakwater. "You can eat clam chowder there, or anything made of clams." And he remembered the couples in the big restaurant on one of the piers. And he remembered himself eating a cup of clam chowder and watching them.

He looked up at Rhea and he was almost surprised that she was there and with him. He smiled and he was grateful.

She grinned and her teeth glistened. "Oh, Jim! You never told me that you had been there."

"That was years ago. It must be different now."

"I'll bet it's just the same. I'll bet we could eat all the clam chowder we ever wanted. . . ."

"And they have a big market there—it's full of vegetables and fish and shops underneath it."

"We could eat all the fish and vegetables. . . ."

"It's beautiful, even in the rain." And when Rhea kissed him and lowered her head to his shoulder, he thought of the couples in the big restaurant. But that was sixteen years ago and he had been a soldier with no place to go. Maybe it *would* be different now, maybe it would be different with someone.

Rhea sighed and sat up. She fluffed her hair. "I have to see to my guests. I wish I could encourage them to just leave. . . ." She sat with her back to him because she had thought of his sister's letter and she felt a little guilty. He has no idea we're batting him back and forth like a Ping-Pong ball, she thought. And I have the advantage now because I'm here. But she would let him think about it for a few days. She didn't want to press her advantage unfairly; she wanted him to be sure. And she knew by now that he scared off easily. But she loved him.

17

Loney looked out the bedroom window and thought for an instant that he had slept through winter. Although there was no sun, a driving warm wind bent the bushes in the yard next door. A woman was hanging out a wash. She was wearing a thin cotton dress and cowboy boots. The dress was blown tight across her body and between her legs. She brushed her hair away from her mouth and hung up a small pair of blue jeans. She had moved in during the summer and she had two small boys and no apparent husband. She wiped the line, then started hanging T-shirts. She couldn't have been more than twenty feet away and Loney noticed the blue veins behind her knees as she bent to her basket. He had never seen her downtown or on the street, just once or twice before in her backyard and she had been hanging out clothes then.

Loney dropped the curtain and finished dressing. He put a clean shirt on inside out but he didn't notice until he tried to button the sleeves. He fixed the shirt, then stepped into his boots. He was still tired, but the sight of the woman had both calmed and cheered him and he didn't know why. He opened the curtain again, but she was gone. Her clothes were flapping wildly and some of the T-shirts had twirled around the line. She had looked like a pleasant woman who had lived a great deal for her years.

Loney put a pot of water on for instant coffee, then he opened the back door. Swipesy sat on the step, his nose high into the wind. Loney reached down and patted him on the shoulder and he jumped, startled at the touch. The dog never barked anymore and Loney thought this was too bad. "Easy, pal," he said and sat down beside him. Swipesy didn't look at him but he leaned against his knee.

The wind was blowing directly from the south and it filled Loney's body with a sharpness it hadn't felt in some time. He shivered, not from the wind but from the sharpness. Then he grew still and his eyes cleared and he saw the rocky shadows of Snake Butte in the distance. It was flat on top and covered with grass. The top looked just like the prairies that surrounded it, but the sides were gunmetal gray and from a distance they looked smooth and sheer. They weren't, though; they were made up of jagged columns of granite and shallow caves. Loney knew this from his childhood, and he also knew about the etchings on the flat stones on top—the crude drawings of deer and fish and lizard. Snake Butte was a perfect fortress and it was assumed that Indian hunters had made the etchings many years ago. Loney used to fish the small reservoir at the base of the butte when he was a kid and he never got over the feeling that there were lives out there. Even now it was not good to think about it.

He breathed in the wind and he felt a sudden tightness in his chest. His shoulders ached and his neck felt knotted up. He hugged Swipesy to his knee and he remembered the drinking and smoking and thinking he had done the week before. And the party at Rhea's. Had that been last night? It must have been. He remembered the people in the living room, then lying in the dark in a small room, then Rhea lying beside him. She had been talking and he had been thinking of Seattle, the mountains and the ferryboats. What did clam chowder have to do with it? The idea made him hungry. He looked into his neighbor's yard and he could see the end of the clothesline. Two shirts had wrapped around each other as though they were desperate friends. Again he thought of Seattle and the whole memory came back: She had wanted him to go to Seattle with her. Just like that. It was beautiful there—trees, rain, the bay, the buildings. He used to watch the ferries. Had he said yes? What about her teaching; had they decided when they would go? Had he said yes? He couldn't have. He couldn't make a decision like that. He needed to think. He wasn't ready to do anything but sit on his step and think, and so he watched the two shirts twist and knot around each other and he thought, not of Seattle, but of the blue veins on the backs of his neighbor's legs.

18

The next day Loney sat up in bed and he felt better. His muscles had relaxed and he didn't think about thinking. He thought about Swipesy. As he swung his legs over the edge of the bed he was surprised to find that he was stiff. His joints ached, but almost righteously so, as though he had done a day's work or had played a good game the night before. He hadn't felt this stiff and achy since his basketball days.

He dressed quickly and walked into the living room. It was furnished with a couch, an overstuffed chair and a glass cabinet. And a dining room table that took up most of the space. Swipesy slept under the table, but he was not there now. Loney glanced at the cabinet and he saw his gold basketball pins, still on cards, and his letter leaning against the back of the top shelf. He had given one of the pins to a girl—Myron Pretty Weasel's sister. He hadn't seen her since one of his furloughs from the army. Margaret. That was her name. She had moved to Billings with her mother while he was gone. Loney wondered what she looked like now. He wondered if she still had his pin. He wondered if she was married and pretty.

He walked through the house, but the dog wasn't around. He opened the back door and looked out into the yard. Then he walked around the house to the street and looked up and down and across to the old apartment building that was being torn down. The lawns were brown and frosty. It was a quiet day, a still day, and the clouds were high and motionless. He turned back to his own house, glancing in the yard next door. The clothes were hanging frozen on the line.

He washed his face and sat down at the kitchen table. He stirred some sugar into his coffee and he noticed the letter leaning against the red candle. It was from Kate, but there was some other writing on the envelope. It read: "I stopped by this morning but you were asleep. Lazybones. Please call me. Love, Rhea."

Loney tore open the envelope and unfolded the paper. "I will be in Havre on the 25th. On the 11:43 plane (Frontier) from Great Falls. You should get this letter in plenty of time to make arrangements to pick me up. If you don't, I'll kill you." Loney glanced at the calendar, but as it happened so often now, he had no idea what the date was.

He found a couple of dollars and some change on the table and put them in his pocket. Then he slipped into his parka and walked downtown. The south wind had died during the night and the ground had hardened up. Loney hated the cold the way some people who had to live on it hated deer meat, hopelessly and without emotion. But today he needed the cold to take away his breath and the ache in his body.

He looked in yards and alleys for Swipesy but without luck, and he knew that Swipesy would not be back.

There was no traffic as he crossed the main street to the Buttrey's store. He got a dozen eggs, a loaf of bread and a quart of milk. Then he picked up two cans of tomato soup. At the checkout stand he asked the clerk what day it was.

She stopped punching the cash register and looked at him. She was small, with red hair and a cheery face, but she didn't seem cheerful.

"It's important to me," Loney said.

"I should think so. It's important to everybody," she said.

"How's that?"

"It's the twenty-fourth. It's Thanksgiving."

Loney looked around the store. Except for him and the checker, it was deserted. He gave her the two dollars and she gave him eleven cents change. She looked as if she was ready to cry.

Loney thanked her. As he pushed open the glass door, she called after him, "Thanksgiving! And I have children!"

19

Thanksgiving and the streets were empty. Loney walked slowly, eating a piece of bread and trying to think what it had been like with his aunt. In the two years he had lived with her, they must have celebrated Thanksgiving, but the only holidays he could remember were Christmas and Easter. He remembered them because of church—midnight mass at Christmas, sunrise service at Easter. He wondered about her men friends because they never seemed to be around on holidays, at least on Christmas and Easter. But maybe they were around on the other holidays; maybe that's why he couldn't remember the other holidays; maybe they took her away with them on Thanksgiving.

Then Loney saw himself and his aunt sitting on the floor, quietly watching the lights on a small tree. It was Christmas Eve and they were drinking cocoa—no, he was drinking cocoa; she was drinking water because she was going to take communion that night—and she lowered her head and started to cry. He was twelve and he put his hand on her hair. He couldn't look at her, but he held his hand there until she stopped. She was good and he moved his fingers through her hair until she stopped. He had felt like a man, and after mass they opened presents and he felt as happy as anyone in the world. She never told him why she had cried and he never asked. It had been enough to feel her hair and smell the Christmas tree. She gave him a pen that wrote in three colors and he gave her a magazine that had beauty secrets, and they ate the pudding that tasted like butterscotch but wasn't.

As he nibbled at the bread, he felt a small regret that she had gone to him. It was no longer a question of a life with her, of a kind of family, which used to fill him with pain; rather, it was a simple regret that he did not get to know her. He wanted to believe that she was beautiful and he wanted to believe that he knew the color of her hair, but he could not, for he didn't know either of these things. The only thing he was sure of was that of all the women in his life, she was the one he had tried hardest to love.

Her name started with an S and she had left and he had been sent away to a mission school in southern Montana. Kate had already left. She had never lived with the aunt. Instead, she had gone away to another mission school, in Flandreau, South Dakota, right after their father had left them. Loney often wondered why she never lived with him and the aunt. It would have been better than any mission school. He had hated his school; he worked hard at his studies, but he hated the dormitory and early morning mass and the pasty cereal. He didn't like the fathers and the brothers—except for Brother Gerard, who taught science and taught him how to play basketball. Loney always believed that it was Brother Gerard who got him sprung too.

It had been in the spring of his second year there. Brother Gerard's class had gone on a field trip to a slough to collect water bugs, and Loney had left the group and followed a cattle trail to the far end of the slough. There, he sat on a beaver-chewed log and stared at the remains of a muskrat that had been trapped but never retrieved. It had crawled up on the bank from the entrance to its hole and its fur was almost gone and its tail had been chewed off. It was leather and bone and past stinking, but it made Loney cry and he thought that he would die, too, if he did not leave that school.

That evening he and Brother Gerard were taking a break after a one-on-one game and Loney told him he had to leave. The brother had sat there on the floor, his back against the folded-up bleachers, in his T-shirt and khaki pants and white sneakers, and he didn't say anything and Loney stood up and walked out on the court and took a last shot—he believed it would be the last shot of his life—and left the gym. But he didn't go back to the dormitory.

They picked him up the next morning on the highway to Billings. He got into a lot of trouble over that, but a couple of weeks later the priest who ran the school told him he had found Loney a place to stay in Harlem. Loney continued in Brother Gerard's science class until the end of the spring term, but they were never close again. Loney never went to the gym and he did not say goodbye when he left.

He lived during his high school years in a boardinghouse run by a minister and his wife. He didn't know much about ministers and he thought it strange that there was no church connected to the boardinghouse. He didn't believe that the man was a real minister. He had no church, and as far as Loney knew, no God. No midnight mass, no sunrise service. Loney did remember saying prayers before meals, but the minister never ate with them. He ate in the kitchen with his wife, after she had served the food to the five or six boys at the table in the dining room. Although the number of boys stayed about the same, the faces changed frequently. Loney outlasted all of them, living at the boardinghouse until the day he graduated. Then he packed his suitcase with his clothes, the small gold basketball pins that he'd won in the three years he played, and the Bible that the minister's wife had given him as a graduation present. He caught the bus up to Havre to enlist in the army and he never saw the minister and his wife again.

As Loney ate his bread and thought about these things, he became aware that he had been watching a small boy squatting beside a rough shape at the edge of an alley. He crossed the street.

The boy stood and stepped back.

"What have you got there?" said Loney.

"Nothing," said the boy.

Swipesy lay on his side, his mouth open and his blind blue eye staring up at nothing. There was something odd in the way he lay, as though he had been split lengthwise. Then Loney saw that he was frozen into the mud.

"What's your name?" he said to the boy.

"Amos," said the boy.

"Can you hold these, Amos?" And Loney handed him the sack of groceries.

Loney tried to lift Swipesy out of the frozen mud, but he had no luck. As he moved his hands down the dog's body, he heard Amos rustling in the sack for a piece of bread. He grabbed two handfuls of Swipesy's fur and tried to lift him. Then he tried the two free legs.

"Can't do it," he said. He stood and looked down at Swipesy, then at Amos. "Damn."

Amos set the groceries on the ground and dug into his coat pocket. Then he handed Loney a knife. It was a fat old pocket-knife with one blade completely gone and the other broken off about half its length.

Loney worked with the broken knife, chipping away flakes of the frozen mud. Once he stopped to rest his hand and said, "How old are you, Amos?"

"My name is Amos After Buffalo."

"This old dog of mine was ready to die, Amos. He was ninety years old."

"I'm seven."

Loney went back to work. He worked carefully, chipping away the mud from around Swipesy's head, then his back, his belly, his legs.

"What are you going to do with him once you get him out?"

"That's a good question."

"Are you going to throw him away?"

"No—I guess I'll bury him."

"That's what I'd do." And Amos After Buffalo squatted to watch. He liked to watch the man work. And he liked being the man's helper. "I'd bury him out there," he said, pointing in the general direction of the Little Rockies.

"Maybe that's just what I'll do."

"That's where I live. I live way out there." He thought for a moment. "Do you know where I live?"

20

Amos After Buffalo stood with the sack of groceries in his arms and watched the man walk away from him. The man cradled the dog the way Amos carried firewood. But today was Thanksgiving and he didn't have to carry logs or anything if he didn't want. He was visiting his aunt and uncle in town and his aunt was cooking a big venison roast. Amos didn't understand Thanksgiving. It was a holiday, but it wasn't like Christmas or Easter or the Fourth of July. It was a time to eat. He wished they had a turkey. A turkey seemed more like a holiday. He had never eaten turkey, but he thought it might be sweet.

Amos After Buffalo watched the man turn the corner at the end of the street. Then he set the groceries down and started to run home. He ran and he thought it was funny that the man didn't seem to be sad about his dog. He had wanted to watch the man bury the dog. But he remembered that his aunt had made a roast and he had been gone for a long time. He would have to break his old record to get home in time.

21

Loney stood behind the old woman and the girl. They were looking out the large windows at the airplane about to land. It came in so slowly and quietly that it seemed to be gliding. Loney could read the letters on the fusilage above the windows—FRONTIER—and he felt a kind of panicky excitement.

The right wheel touched the ground first, sending up a spray of blue smoke; then the left wheel touched, and finally the nose wheel settled on the runway. Suddenly the roar of the engines shook the windows of the little terminal and the old woman took a step back, almost bumping into Loney. She wore an old cloth coat and a black silk scarf and moccasins and leggings. Loney guessed that she was from Rocky Boy, because the old women still dressed that way out there. The girl was wearing a blue parka and checkered slacks and white sneakers. She looked to be about fifteen or sixteen. She stared with awe at the airplane, which was taxiing toward the gate. She hadn't noticed that her grandmother was now standing directly behind her, between her and Loney. The grandmother was frightened at the sight of the large plane bearing down on the terminal, but she didn't show it. She seemed impassive, and as Loney looked down at her shoulders and her silver, yellowing hair, he thought, That's the way old Indian women get; they've seen so much in their years, so many of these winters. . . .

The left engine came to a stop and a door behind the cockpit opened. Metal stairs slowly unfolded and lowered to the pavement.

Loney patted his hair down. He had got it cut that morning in Harlem and it felt slick and neat. He had also shaved and put on his best white shirt. He was excited because he knew that Kate would be perfect. He always loved to look at her and her beauty always affected him and he knew it was because he hadn't seen much of her since he was ten and she was fifteen. Now she was like a beautiful stranger to him until they got reacquainted. He had seen her only four or five times, all in the last ten years, since they parted as children. He had last seen her three years ago and he remembered how she looked—tall, willowy, maybe a little skinny, but no skinnier than some of the magazine models Loney had looked at. And he remembered the high wide cheekbones, which gave her face a soft diamond shape that he found lovely and strong.

Again he wondered why she had never married. He wondered that a lot, at odd moments. Sometimes he thought it was because of her job: she was just too busy flying around the country, telling people what to do and how to do it. At other times he thought it was because she was too strong. He couldn't imagine any man being equal to her. He smiled because he had been dreading this moment all morning for just that reason. But now he was excited. He knew that they would get reacquainted and everything would be fine. She would be his sister again.

A man carrying a briefcase emerged first, hurrying down the stairs without looking up, as though he expected to be taken for a celebrity. An elderly couple followed him, waving toward the terminal, but as far as Loney could tell, only he and the old woman and the girl were waiting. Then a young Indian in a green army uniform got off. His hat was back on his head and his tie was loose. He looked as if he had been traveling for days. The girl said something in Cree to the old woman and they moved toward the boarding area. Loney continued to stare at the door behind the cockpit. Nobody appeared for a few moments. Then a stewardess emerged from the darkness and descended the stairs. She was carrying a clipboard, holding it up to shield her hair from the slight wind. Loney could see a gold bracelet on her slender wrist.

He waited a while longer. Then he walked over to the Frontier counter, but there was no one around. He read the schedule board: FLIGHT 71, 11:43 A.M. The clock at the far end of the building said 11:48. It had to be the right plane.

The stewardess had walked up to the counter and was writing something on the clipboard.

"Excuse me," said Loney. "Did everybody who was supposed to get off that plane get off?"

The stewardess glanced out the window at the plane. Then she looked at her clipboard. "Four passengers . . . Um hum, yes."

"But my sister . . ."

"Was she by any chance coming from the south?"

"Arizona."

"Okay, um hum, I understand. It's been happening all day. Sir, the Denver airport has been closed because of blizzard conditions. I assume she would have had to change planes in Denver. But she was probably rerouted to Salt Lake, in which case"—she squinted at the schedule board—"she'll probably catch a later flight to Billings and connect up with our flight forty-three, which comes in here at five-thirty."

"You mean she'll be here later today?"

"Unless her plane landed in Denver. Some planes landed there earlier this morning. But all traffic is grounded now and likely will be for the rest of the day. I wouldn't worry. She probably went on to Salt Lake. You just be here at five-thirty." She smiled and walked briskly toward the boarding gate.

Loney watched her until she passed the soldier and the girl

and the old woman. Then he watched them. They had their arms around each other; rather, the soldier had his arms around them and the girl had her arms around him. They both had their heads bowed as though they were saying a prayer. The old woman had her arms at her sides, accepting the soldier's hug. She was thinking that it was a bad world when her grandson comes home to her on a machine that flies. Later, when he told her stories of where he had been and what he had seen, she would realize that she had lost him. She sensed this now and it filled her with sadness, for she knew that what he had gained would never make up for what he had lost. She had seen the other boys come home. And she stared past her soldier at Loney's wolfish face and she thought, That's one of them.

22

Loney sat in his car in the parking lot all afternoon. The morning clouds had dissipated and the sky was a brilliant blue and the sun warmed the car. The car was a '64 Chevy and it had started that morning without hesitation, much to Loney's surprise. Having forgotten almost everything of small consequence, he couldn't remember when he had driven it last. He had put a blanket over the seat to hide the holes that mice had chewed in the fabric.

The sun came through the windshield and it made him drowsy and he dozed off, but he didn't know for how long. Once he started the car and began to drive toward town for a bite to eat, or a bottle of wine, or just the drive—he didn't know which—but he had turned around and driven back to the airport. He didn't like Havre and he knew he had better not drink. Thinking of Kate, he grew excited again.

She was not on the five-thirty plane. The man behind the counter was no help. He thought maybe the Salt Lake City airport had been closed too, but he didn't know. He just knew there was a blizzard in the southern Rockies. He began to switch off the lights.

Loney thought of calling Rhea because she would know what to do, she was good that way, but he thought better of it. There was a chance that she might bring up the Seattle business and he couldn't handle it. He wasn't ready. And for the time being, Kate was the only important woman in his life. He didn't have enough of himself to give to both of them.

He felt weak. He knew he should eat, but the only thing he wanted was a bottle of wine. And some cigarettes. In truth he desired neither, but he thought he did, and the thought was enough. He started the car and drove down to the main highway that would take him into Havre, and he hoped to some sort of controlled oblivion, if such a state existed.

2

Painter Barthelme stepped between the two Indians and pushed the smaller one back over a stool. The stool fell and the man fell with it, hitting his head hard on the floor. He moaned and rolled over and held the back of his head. The fight had gone out of him for the moment.

Painter turned to the other man and said, "Now what the hell is this all about?"

"He attacked me," said the other man. He was big and drunk, but not drunk enough to take chances with.

Painter kept his hand on his holster and tried to gauge the man's eyes. "Come on," he said. "Tell it to me straight."

"I mean it. Pepion tried to kill me," said the big Indian. "Jesus, two drinks and he turns into Superman. Look at the bastard."

Pepion was pulling himself up by the rungs of a bar stool. Painter grabbed him by the arm and jerked him to his feet. "Are you all right?" he said.

"Where is that fucker?" said Pepion. His right eye had closed and his face was red and puffy. His lip was split right under his nose.

Painter turned to the big Indian. "Did you do this?" It was a silly question and Painter almost sighed.

"He came after me. I don't know what the hell came over him. I was just sitting here with Waker. He'll tell you. Ain't it, Waker?"

Waker laughed. "We was just sitting here." Waker was still sitting there. "We was just talking about our careers."

"That's right, officer. We've been thinking of starting up our own bowling alley. We'd just got to the part about the cocktail lounge—see, we want to have our own cocktail lounge right in the bowling alley—and this damn Pepion goes berserk."

"Any idea why?"

"We was just saying that we didn't think we should allow Indians in. High-class, you see." Waker winked at the big Indian.

"It's not that we're prejudiced," said the big Indian. He turned to the bar and reached for his bottle of beer, but it lay on its side, its contents still moving like lava down the bar.

"Goddamn you, Pepion," said the big Indian. He made a fist and stepped forward.

Pepion fell backward over the stool that lay on the floor. This time he grabbed his left elbow and moaned as though his heart would break.

"Now look at that! You saw it—I didn't touch him. Ain't it, Waker? See what I mean?"

Painter again helped Pepion to his feet. He held him up and turned to the big Indian. "That's enough. Now get the hell out of here. Take that other ignorant bastard with you."

"But it's a free country," protested Waker.

"Not for you it isn't. Now go on. You've got five seconds before I run you across the street. Goddamn your hides."

Painter watched them hurry out the door. He knew it wasn't because they were afraid of him. It was Friday afternoon and they wanted to remain free men for the night ahead. He would probably see them again. He turned to Pepion. "I'd better get you over to the agency hospital. Get that lip sewed up."

"Look at my fingers." Pepion held out his hand. "I can't even move 'em. I'm gonna sue those fuckers."

Painter helped Pepion out the door and into his cruiser. He closed the door and looked at his watch. Jesus, two o'clock and I've already got my first casualty. What a country. He walked around the car and got in. Pepion was already nodding off. "Now don't go to sleep on me, Pepion. I thought you were going to sue those fuckers." But Pepion's head jerked and hit the window. He slumped down in the seat and was gone.

Just like a baby, thought Painter. Goddamn country. He should have stayed in California . . . he shouldn't have let that woman run him out. It was always women with him. He watched his face in the rear-view mirror as he clasped his shoulder harness. It was a handsome face, a real California-rugged cowboy face with crow squints and droopy mustache. He smiled and shook his head. His face always made him feel better. He started the car and backed out onto the street.

2

Kate Loney walked briskly across the tarmac apron toward the terminal. She strode past the other passengers, each of whom turned to look at her with upstaged curiosity, but she seemed unaware of them. In her thick-soled boots she was six feet tall, lean and striking as a dark cat. Her black hair was pulled back from her face and clasped neatly behind her head with a beaded roach. Her necklace was squash blossom, turquoise and silver, and her earrings were silver hoops. She wore a turquoise blouse and a black skirt that came halfway down her calves, and over that, a sheepskin jacket. She looked as if she couldn't decide what to wear and so she wore a bit of everything. And in truth, she had been a little deliberate about choosing each piece of clothing. She didn't want to intimidate her brother with one of her city outfits, so she had bought the sheepskin jacket in a Western boutique in Phoenix. She was a little disgusted with herself for that move, but the squash blossom was authentic, right from the heart of Navaho country. She had bought it directly from the woman who made it. She was the only woman silversmith in the Canyon de Chelly area. No middleman. Kate felt righteous about that one.

She was a day late and she hoped her brother knew about the snowstorm in Denver. The plane from Phoenix had been able to land but no flights got off the ground after that, so she had spent the night in a Ramada Inn next to the airport. She had been annoyed at first, but after she got settled in she had found herself enjoying the night's isolation. It always surprised her, when she was on the road, how pleasant it could be without people, to lie half naked on a queen-size bed and watch a couple of hours of silly shows on the television. It seemed to her at those moments that her life had been drained from her body, and last night it was all she could do to turn back the sheet and crawl into bed. She had poured a glass of Scotch from her traveling flask, but she hadn't the energy to drink it. Usually a Scotch revived her, but last night it didn't have a chance.

As she strode toward the terminal she felt good, renewed, joyful and annoyed. She loved her brother more than anything, but she had gotten used to hiding this feeling, not out of awkwardness or reserve, but because it almost broke her heart to think of him. And thinking this, she was annoyed because she knew from past experience that he wouldn't be there.

She looked at the terminal window for the first time and felt her heart lift as she looked into her brother's wolfish face, so hungry and shy that she became giddy.

And as she hugged his thin body, she breathed in the sour, smoky odor of bars and booze and she didn't care. She heard him say, "I waited for you," and she said, "Yes, you did, didn't you?"

And he said, "I thought about going home but I waited for you."

When he said it a third time, she realized that he was absolutely smashed, but she didn't even mind that much. She was here and she knew what to do. She sat him down and put her leather briefcase on his lap. Then she walked over to the car rental counter. She didn't bother to ask him if he had brought his. She handed the girl her American Express card and she looked out toward the airplane which was taxiing toward the runway and she thought, Perhaps by this time next week both of us . . . But she didn't allow herself to complete her thought. Bad luck; she didn't need it.

3

"What shall we do today?"

Kate watched the soapy water swirl down the drain. The breakfast dishes glistened in a rack beside her. She was happy and at peace with this small world. It seemed so simple and logical—no planes, no appointments, no calls to return, no stacks of paper. It was just this—breakfast dishes and a free day. She looked out the window to the yard next door and she smiled. I'm the one who's supposed to convince him that he should come back to Washington with me, and all I can think of is how peaceful his life is.

And it had been a perfect three days. The morning after their drive down from Havre, Loney had got up and gone to the store for groceries. By the time Kate staggered into the kitchen, still exhausted from the accumulation of her life, he had cleaned it and was starting breakfast. He hadn't seemed to be hung over at all. He had been fresh, and a little apologetic. Until she hugged him.

Now she looked at the frozen clothes on the line next door

and she wished they could both have a life like this, but she knew they couldn't. She needed her work and he needed something. He would start drinking again as soon as she left, and so it was important that she keep her goal fixed.

But she was happy and she felt her brother's eyes on her, and she knew that for a change a man, a young man, was watching her without a trace of desire or lust or whatever. He was simply watching her. She had become used to the men in Washington and the men she met on the road. Most of them were business associates in one way or another, but when the business was done and the inevitable cocktails flowed, they became randy and full of themselves. The men on the road were the worst. They seemed to think of her as a sex-starved gypsy and imagined they were there to satisfy her as no other man could. She had become an expert at recognizing that precise moment when the good fellowship ended and the lust began. And she knew that she was asking for it, not by innuendo or suggestion but by the nature of things, a woman in a man's world and so on and on. If you were the least bit attractive you became the object of their fuck game. And you became cynical.

"What shall we do today?"

She turned from the sink and wiped her hands on a dish towel. She pretended to be trying to make up her mind, but she really didn't care. If they just sat at the table and talked all day, that would be good enough with her. But she did have to call her office sometime. She frowned as though she were thinking hard. "Let's see. What if we had a cigarette and a cup of coffee, then went downtown—I have to call in—and we could just walk around for a while. I want to see if Harlem has changed in my absence. Then . . . we could go meet your girl. That's it. We'll go meet Rhea. I want to know who you've been hanging around with."

Kate poured the coffee and she became thoughtful. She had been watching and listening to Loney very carefully during the past three days to see if he had any idea that she had come to take him back to Washington with her. But nothing he said indicated that he knew or even suspected. Which meant that Rhea hadn't mentioned it to him. And this disturbed her. She had made it clear that she wanted Rhea to soften him up. Why hadn't she? She couldn't want him to stay here, knowing that he was on his way to self-destruction.

There were several things about Rhea Davis that Kate wanted to find out. What did she look like? How did she conduct herself? Why had she come all the way up here from Texas? But Kate wanted to know most of all what Rhea had found in her brother. Why would a "respectable" schoolteacher find Loney significant, not to mention worth saving?

The sun had appeared for the first time through the broken morning clouds and it came in the window and bathed the small white table. Kate set the coffeepot back on the stove and she looked at her brother, and she thought, There is something about that face like a wolf, so canny and innocent, that is attractive, and she wondered if Rhea's experiences with men weren't something like her own. She didn't like herself to think like this, so she thought instead of the sunlight on her brother's hand.

4

Rhea opened the door and she touched her heart and said, "Oh, my," for the resemblance of the two people was unmistakable. Later, when she had a chance to study them, she would find the sister beautiful and the brother fascinating in comparison, as if she hadn't really looked at him before, but now she gasped, "Oh, my!"

"I'm Kate." And Kate extended her hand.

Rhea took the hand and did a little dip and said, "You must forgive me. I'm Rhea." Then she looked at Loney and laughed. "Hi there. Oh!"

"Hello," said Loney, smiling and feeling far off. He felt far off and he realized that he had missed her, and as he looked into her turquoise eyes, as deep and flat as a cat's, he knew that she had missed him. His hands trembled and he held them against his thighs.

And Rhea was saying, "Isn't it a lovely day, come in, I was just sitting by the window," and Kate was saying, "You have a wonderful view of Snake Butte, don't bother, and look, the Bearpaws. . . ."

Loney sat down on the graceful leather couch and watched the two women at the window. He was a little stunned. He had never thought that the three of them would one day be together. Why that seemed so momentous he couldn't say, but as he looked at them he felt like a third party. He lit a cigarette with the big crystal lighter and his hands were trembling.

Kate turned from the window and said, "You beast, you don't even care about the view."

And Rhea laughed and said, "Oh, Jim!"

"Isn't he awful?"

"The pits."

Loney smiled at the two women, one tall and dark, the other small and fair, both wonderfully pretty, and he thought, It is a fine view, I'm happy enough. And he was suddenly quite happy.

"I just got home myself—from school. I was just going to put on some tea water. Or would you rather have wine?"

"No," Kate said. "The tea will be fine. Are you sure we're not disturbing you?"

"How could you? I've been dying to meet you."

"Well, I've heard all manner of things about you from this one here."

"All bad, I'm sure."

"Hardly."

After Rhea left the room, Kate said, "She's lovely. Oh, and that Southern drawl! Miss Scarlett O'Hara." She rolled her eyes the way she imagined a Negro mammy might, but she was troubled more than ever. Rhea was lovely and well-bred. So why Harlem? And why her brother?

"She is lovely," Loney said, looking into the fireplace and thinking of his dark bird and the night it had appeared there.

"How long have you known her? I forget."

"I don't remember. I didn't know her for a long time."

"But how did you meet?"

Loney thought of the basketball game. That seemed like years ago. "She was selling tickets and I bought one from her. She hates basketball."

Rhea returned with a small silver plate. "I'm afraid these are just old store-bought cookies. I never seem to get around to baking."

Kate said, "You have a very distinctive accent. It didn't come through in your letter."

Rhea laughed. "That's what my students tell me. Sometimes I just hate it. It sounds awful to me."

"But it's lovely," Kate protested.

"Letter?"

Both women looked at him. Then Kate glanced at Rhea and she knew that Rhea hadn't mentioned her letter or her plan. She was momentarily confused. Then she said, "We exchanged letters, just to get to know each other," and saying it, realized that they—she and Rhea—were in competition and they had been competing since that exchange. What had seemed so clear to Kate before was becoming clouded by this idea of competition. Long-distance, no less. And what a funny competition, the prize being her brother. She couldn't believe that Rhea would want him. She had her own world, back there in Texas, and she couldn't possibly want Jim Loney. She will leave here, thought Kate, probably at the end of the school year; she can't take this place, this life. And what will become of my brother? Rhea can't wish this life on him. She must know I've got to get him away.

Her thoughts were interrupted by her brother's voice. "I might have a glass of wine, if that's okay."

Rhea looked at Kate and Kate nodded. "I'll have some too." She thought it would be best to drink with him.

"Then we'll all have wine. It is a celebration, isn't it?"

5

Kenny Hart watched Ike try to strike up a conversation with the young Indian woman. She was small and dark and she wore too much makeup. Beneath that paint and powder, her face was calm and graceful, almost pious, and Kenny thought that she looked an awful lot like Ike's ex-wife. And Kenny thought it remarkable that this girl would come in on a random winter night and make him think of Ike's wife. After forty years, more or less. Eletra. That was her name. She drove them wild until she left Ike and then they drove her crazy. Kenny was half in love with her himself. He and Ike worked together then, for ranchers and farmers up and down the valley, and so he saw a lot of her. But Kenny had always been an honorable man and he never joined the crowd that flocked around Eletra. Not even after she and Ike split up, none too gracefully. A couple of years later she just went crazy. A combination of booze and an excess of men. Kenny heard that she was still down in the state hospital in Warm Springs. He also heard that she was in prison in Nebraska. And he heard she went up to Alaska to work with the Eskimos. She had been a nurse before she met Ike.

The young woman looked away toward the pool table, where the two men she had come in with were having a game. Kenny didn't know them. From their slacks and tight shirts he guessed that they were from Great Falls or Billings. Christ, the shorter one was even wearing a necklace. But he looked mean and Kenny figured he'd better warn Ike off. He polished his glasses on his apron, then reached under the bar for the brick he'd found that day. It was red and had three holes in a line. He threw it on the bar in front of Ike.

"Know what this is?"

Ike Loney stopped in midsentence and glared at Kenny.

"Take a chance." Kenny picked the brick up and held it before Ike's eyes.

"A brick?" said Ike.

"A North Dakota bowling ball." Kenny waited for Ike to catch on.

But Ike frowned and turned to the woman again and said, "Let me just buy you one drink, a friendly drink. What's the matter with that?"

Kenny sighed and threw the brick under the bar. Poor old bastard. She probably reminds him of Eletra too, although his memories of her can't be too fond. Kenny had watched Ike change from a young rowdy to a bitter man. Eletra started it, but his kids finished it. When she ran off and left him with those kids, that finished it. He had become mean, and then bitter. And then he took off. That was the one thing Kenny could never forgive Ike. How he left those kids. But they were still friends of a sort, or at least Kenny pitied him enough to support his drinking, and Ike had once been a good man and a hell of a companion.

Kenny had an old candy box full of pictures at home and sometimes after a rough shift, he would drag it out and remind himself that once there was a future for the likes of Ike Loney and Clancy Peters. One photo that he was especially fond of showed Clancy, him and Ike standing in front of the bucking chutes down at the fairgrounds in Dodson. There was nothing in the world that those three rowdies couldn't do, from fighting to riding, to drinking, to loving. Now Clancy had sugar diabetes and a loud-mouthed woman and Ike had nothing, except a couple of kids he didn't know. And I've got a bar, thought Kenny, and he was grateful for that. Most of the time he didn't need any more than that.

He popped another Oly and set it in front of Ike. "Putting it on your tab, old-timer." He walked back to the till and made an imaginary notation on a piece of paper.

The two Great Falls men had finished their game and were sparring with the wall.

"I like it hot!" one said.

"I like it shiny!" said the other.

"I like it hot and shiny!"

Goddamn, thought Kenny, it could have been a good peaceful night. And he hoped to hell that Ike would quit fooling around with that girl.

One of the Great Falls men slammed his palm on the bar. "Hey, what the fuck?" he yelled. "You running a bar here or not?"

Kenny opened the beers and he thought, Thirty-five, forty years ago, me and Ike would have given these punks all they wanted. He pushed his glasses up on the hump of his mostly flattened nose.

"Hey, what the fuck?" yelled the other Great Falls man. "You running a drinking establishment or not?"

Kenny set the beers on the bar. His numbing stick was by his knee, within reach. "That'll be one-eighty, boys," he said.

6

Painter Barthelme pulled his cruiser to the curb and switched off the engine. He zipped up his jacket. He was feeling good. His lecture to the high school students that afternoon had gone off without a hitch. Sometimes it pays to be a cop. That afternoon it had paid. He could see just the right amount of fear in their eyes and he had made sure it stayed there with stories of high-speed chases and desperate shoot-outs. Of course, it was against the department's policy to talk of such things. He was supposed to be a goodwill ambassador, not a messenger of death and destruction. But he had passed his badge around and he had handcuffed the teacher to the radiator and he had told them that he could be their friend, he wanted to be their friend. But he just couldn't help putting a little fear into them. And the siren had been a stroke of genius. By the time he pulled up to the school there were twenty people running out the door to see what was up. He had got their attention.

Painter thought again of the teacher he had handcuffed to the radiator. He'd been thinking of her all evening. He couldn't believe that they hadn't crossed paths before and she hadn't worn a wedding ring and that was a novelty in this town. It was the first thing he noticed about her. He had a good eye when it came to women. But what was really unique about her was her accent, that Southern drawl. It was unexpected and thrilling the way she'd said, "Oh, you," when she realized she was his prisoner. It was like the students weren't there, the way she'd said it, as though they'd shared an intimate joke. She was small and blond and his prisoner. Painter had had a number of women since he came up from California four years ago. Some of them were women he could lose his job over, pillars of society, and that was a laugh. But this one was different. He got out of the cruiser and walked down the sidewalk toward the Serviceman's. It was a cold clear night. He touched his holster and smiled. He'd kept her cuffed to the radiator longer than he'd planned, at least ten minutes, and the students loved it. They'd had no idea how much he loved it.

7

Rhea put the last of the evening's dishes into the dishwasher. She was sad and elated. So many things ran through her mind that she couldn't catch any of them. She tried to remember exactly that evening's conversation. She tried to remember the various looks on Kate's face as the evening and the wine wore on. And she tried to remember if Loney had given any indication that he had decided to go to Seattle with her. And she wondered if she had decided to go to Seattle. She probably would—she would—if he came with her. But alone? Without knowing a soul?

She remembered the bath water and she ran down the hall to her bedroom. She got there just in time. The water was an inch from the rim of the tub and scalding hot. My God, she sighed. And as she undressed she thought of a prayer that a girlfriend had taught her when she was seven: "Angel of God, my guardian dear, whom God sent to protect me here, ever this day be at my side, to light and guard, to rule and guide." Rhea had said this every day for five years, until her mother found out it was a Catholic prayer. It was a lovely prayer, but henceforth forbidden. Now she said it.

And she hung her suit on a hanger, then slipped off her half slip, her panties and bra. In a way, she felt that she was in a forbidden situation again. She sought to throw herself between brother and sister. That's a mighty dramatic verb, she thought. Insinuate is more to the point. And she didn't like the sound of it. She needed to talk to Kate. But she didn't know how to arrange it. Kate was leaving in three days.

She drained some of the water from the tub and turned on the cold water. She waited a few seconds, then she stepped into the water, feeling the hot and cold mix around her leg. She liked Kate. She loved the way she looked, the way she wore jewelry, her long fingers. Sometimes when she was around beautiful women, she felt small and awkward, but Kate was different—she was earthy, talky, even a little wicked, and Rhea felt that they could be friends. After all, they had the same goal, to get Loney away from there. If either of them won, they should both be happy.

As Rhea lowered herself into the water, she felt her breasts get light, and she thought, But it goes a little beyond the common good. It goes to the heart. She watched her toes turn pink in the hot water and she wondered if she was justified in trying to keep Loney. She remembered her feelings about him that night a year ago when they first made love. She had been surprised that he was so quiet and gentle, yet strong. Not like the men she had made love with before. Maybe it was a Texas trait, she thought as the water made her arms weak, that need to display aggression as though they were roosters pinning down a hen. Silly, she chided herself, one of the men was a Jew from New York. Maybe she had just been unlucky. And she wondered when her relationship with Loney had changed from simple sex to love. Had it? Yes, she was sure of that. She did love him and she was quite sure that he loved her. Sometimes they were perfect lovers—the trouble was Rhea never knew when those times would occur. Complications. And to think I came north to escape them, she thought. She ran the washcloth over her face and smiled. Maybe those Texas men weren't so bad after all. Oh, lord. And she laughed out loud.

8

"I don't understand you."

"I know. I don't understand myself."

They walked on in silence. They were on the last street on the eastern edge of town. They could see the lights of the agency four miles away through the trees that marked the Milk River. The stars were bright and severely patterned and Loney remembered the summer nights that Kate had taught him stars and constellations. In those days he could never quite see the order. It was all high chaos to him.

"Did you know I came all the way out here to take you back with me?"

"I guess not. I mean, I should have guessed. I guess I'm not very smart. I should have known from your letters."

"I can't believe you didn't know."

"I'm not as smart as some people."

"Don't say that!" Kate snapped. "Don't ever say that. You're as smart as anybody." Then she added: "Unfortunately, you don't seem to know it."

They were walking beside a barbed-wire fence. Out in the field Loney could see the cattle. They were black Angus and they looked like similar dark stones. None moved.

"I don't understand what you expect to happen to you here. Do you think that one day you're going to wake up and things will be different? You'll suddenly have something, be something?"

"What would I have there?"

Kate stopped and touched his arm. "Everything. Some good and some bad. But you would have things worthwhile. I could be modest but I won't: you would have me, your sister. And other things—things you can't imagine: beautiful country, a city, the North, the South, the ocean. . . . You need that. You need things to be different, things that would arouse your curiosity, give you some purpose. For God's sake, I've been here four days and I've seen how you live. Don't misunderstand—I've had a wonderful peaceful time—but you can't go on day after day sitting at that table, looking out that window. What will you do when I'm gone? I'm afraid to even think about it."

Loney looked down at his sister's chest and he wanted to say that it wasn't that bad, that he had been thinking and it was going to take some time. After that he would be free.

One of the cattle started walking away from the others, farther out into the field. And the other cattle moved as one heartbeat to follow.

Loney said, "I've got Rhea." He hoped his sister would accept this as a kind of solution.

But Kate said, "For how long? God, sometimes I envy you. You live in a fool's paradise."

"That's okay," said Loney. "She loves me."

"And she'll take care of you? Listen, she has her own world. I don't know anything about her background, but you can damn well bet that she comes from a world as foreign to you as Mars. What happens to you when she decides to go back, when she decides that her little fling with Harlem is over? Oh, I hoped that you would at least be able to see that." Kate started walking again. She walked fast and Loney had to trot to catch up.

"She cares for me," he said.

"We all care for you, and that's the trouble." Kate stopped again. Loney almost bumped into her. "God, I wish we'd grown up differently, together. When we were kids I taught you things and you learned them. You were so smart then." She turned her head away and Loney knew she was crying.

He put his arm around her and patted her shoulder, but she wouldn't come close. He knew she wouldn't. They were both awkward now.

"Look! Did you see that? A shooting star."

He felt Kate's shoulder jump beneath his hand, then again, and he heard her laugh. "You didn't see anything, you dope."

"I did. I swear it. Over there." And he pointed to the southern sky. It was an old joke. When they were kids and Kate pointed out the stars to him, he would suddenly see a shooting star. It was the only way he could get to her. They used to argue violently over his sudden sightings.

"Oh, let's go home. I have a flask of Scotch. Tonight I need a drink worse than you do." Kate wiped her eyes with the sleeve of her sheepskin jacket. "Will you promise me one thing? Promise me that you won't say positively no yet. Will you give me these last three days to try to convince you to come with me?"

Loney said, "Yes," but he didn't understand his sudden popularity. He had lived most of his life in Harlem, and now two different people wanted him to leave with them. He had been stupid. Every one of his sister's letters had ended with the offer to pay his way back to Washington, D.C., but he had always considered that a refrain, a way to end the letters politely, the way some people ended conversations by saying "Take care of yourself."

Loney looked back toward the field, but a street light flattened his vision and he couldn't see the cattle like stones.

"I promise," he said. And he wondered if he should tell Kate about Rhea's plans for him.

9

"Jesus Christ, you're just in time."

Painter stood inside the door and unzipped his jacket. He raised his head and he could see his breath. "In time for what?"

"To avoid all the trouble. You timed it perfectly."

"You had some trouble?"

"Did we have some trouble, Ike? Did I just kick two assholes and their woman the hell out of here? Did I just threaten them with extinction? Or was that all my imagination? Tell him, Ike."

"Aw, hell," said Ike. He was down in the dumps.

"No—there were two guys from Great Falls in here. Tried to get fresh. I gave them the bum's rush, couldn't have been more than three minutes ago. Isn't that right, Ike?"

But Ike stared at the beer before him.

"He's just being moody. Pay no attention to him. He tried to put the make on their woman. Can you imagine that? You should be ashamed of yourself, Ike, an old fart like you."

Painter sat down at the bar.

"You off shift?"

He looked at his watch. It was twelve-ten. He smiled sweetly at Kenny and said, "You fucking' A."

"That's the idea. Here, let me pour you one. This is my private stock. Let me know what you think."

Painter picked up the shot glass, sniffed it, then threw it

back. When he recovered, he said, "Holy shit! What the hell is that? I'd hate to see what you serve to ordinary citizens."

"Jesus. Ordinary citizens. How about that, Ike?"

Painter looked around the bar. "Give me another." The place was empty except for him and Kenny and Ike, but he wished he had changed out of his uniform. And there was the cruiser. He wasn't used to working the swing shift, but that fucking Myers was sick again.

"How about a little cribbage? Dime a point. I'll spot you anything you want, you name it."

"What is this stuff?"

"Rum. One-eighty proof. Take the chill off the balls of a brass monkey. Hey, you know the definition of an Eskimo with a hard-on? A frigid midget with a rigid digit."

"Wouldn't have to be an Eskimo. Cold enough out there to freeze a witch's tit."

"Ha ha. That's a good one, Barthelme. You should have been a comedian. I'll have to remember that one. I haven't heard that one since the sixth grade. Dime a point. I need to get a little of that tax money back."

"Kenny, I ought to run your ass in. Every time you open your mouth you're disturbing the peace."

"Whoops. Okay. I'm not even smiling now. Hey, Ike, am I smiling?"

But Ike wasn't listening to them. He picked at the label on his beer and thought of the woman he had just talked to. For a few moments he had been taken back to a time he had spent forty years forgetting. Eletra. Usually the thought of her made him sad, then agitated, then outraged. But that young woman—even with her makeup and her aloofness, she reminded him of Eletra in the good days before the kids came, when they spent all their time in bars. And the thought made him sad, but those few moments with the girl had made him happy and just a little goofy, like he was a young man again. Then Kenny came along with that goddamn brick. He should have asked her her name. It wouldn't have surprised him if it was Eletra. Nothing would surprise him. Those two punks she was with—that was Eletra all over again. And now he felt the rage build inside him and he blocked out the rest of it and he tried to hang on to a memory the girl had evoked of Eletra when times were good and there was just the two of them. He had seen it for a few shaky moments.

"Here you go, old man." Kenny set a cold beer before Ike and he watched him. Ike lifted his eyes. "Are you all right?" Kenny said, and Ike said, "You and that goddamn brick."

10

Loney stepped from the alley and hurried half a block to the liquor store. Myron Pretty Weasel watched him from the cab of his pickup. He had the heater going and Hank Williams's 24 Greatest Hits on the tape deck. He was still as lean and powerful as the day he played his last basketball game down in Wyoming. That was fifteen years ago.

Pretty Weasel was doing very well for himself. He had made the right decision to give up college and come home to go in with his dad. Now they had the biggest spread on the reservation and he had been responsible for that. He had learned enough business in college to run the ranch right, and he had learned about ranching, not from his father, but from some of the bigger operators, the white men from down the valley. He had learned about pregnancy testing and selling off the drys and buying heifers; he had learned about leveling his hayfields, diking and ditching for irrigation; and he had learned how to manipulate a couple of the tribal councilmen, which made many things possible, including leases and loans to expand his holdings. It was Pretty Weasel's aim to take the guesswork out of ranching. The only problem he had was with the cattle market itself, which was as low as it had been in fifteen years. But they weren't in trouble yet. He ran a tight operation and his father left him alone.

He and his father lived by themselves. His mother and two older sisters had pulled out a long time ago and gone to Billings to live. He saw them occasionally, about once a year when he went to Billings on business, but the divided family stayed pretty much apart. His mother, who was a grade school principal now, had never asked for money, and his father (lately Myron himself) had never offered any.

It had been in his junior year in college, just before basketball season, that the women had left. And he made up his mind in the course of one rambling afternoon to come home. He told no one at Wyoming that he was leaving. He had a car by this time and he packed it with his clothes and hi-fi set and drove home. It was during this drive, just at the Montana border, among aspens and pines, that it occurred to him to feel free, to feel that he had made his first decision and it had been the right one. It didn't matter that the decision was just to come home—now, when he looked back on it, he realized that it hadn't been a decision at all, it was more an automatic response, the way a sheepdog returns to camp in the evening. What mattered was that he did it. As he descended the pass into Montana, he realized how childish his life had been and the act of leaving it behind became as irreversible as death in his mind. To put a ball through a steel hoop with a net hanging from it: that life had ended at that moment.

Loney walked into the liquor store, first looking up and down the street as though someone was after him. Pretty Weasel turned down the tape and smiled in the dark of the cab. There was something about Loney that hadn't changed and it had to do with that quick animal glance, always alert, yet seeming to see nothing. He had been the best ball handler and passer that Pretty Weasel had played with or against. He never looked at you but he always got the ball to you, even when you didn't expect it. Sometimes when you saw him just right, his face was exactly that of a mongrel, hungry and unpredictable, yet funny-looking. Once in a game Pretty Weasel had broken toward the free-throw line and Loney had looked right at him before passing and Pretty Weasel fell in love right on the spot. He started laughing and the ball went through his hands and hit him in the face. He had gotten a bloody nose out of it, but he always considered that moment one of the high points of his career.

He had almost seen that look just now and he wondered how he and Loney could have drifted apart so absolutely. Loney was the last friend he'd had. Now he was gone, into the liquor store, into some kind of desperado life that had nothing to do with Myron Pretty Weasel. And he saw the irony in the fact that he had become the solid citizen and Loney the derelict. All through high school Loney had been the smart one, the one they all got their answers off, the one who lived in that proper boardinghouse run by the preacher. What happened?

Pretty Weasel turned up the tape. Hank Williams was singing "I'm so lonesome I could die."

11

Rhea opened her locker in the teachers' lounge and she was mildly surprised to find so little in it. She had two weeks until the end of the term, but she had been thinking all day about leaving. And she thought she should start cleaning out her locker. She would do it little by little to escape attention. She wasn't ready yet to tell Mr. Gaetano, the principal. He would raise hell. He was an old tyrant.

But after two years her locker was virtually empty. The contents were pitiful and she almost laughed. An umbrella, a box of Tampax, a gym suit and a pair of white sneakers. She put on her coat and stocking cap and she dropped the gym clothes and Tampax in her briefcase.

"What kind of a day did you have?"

Rhea turned as Colleen closed the teachers' lounge door. Then she bent down and snapped her briefcase shut. "Exasperating," she said.

"Don't let the bastards wear you down. What's the Latin for that, anyway?"

Rhea laughed. "I don't know. Right now my mind is a bog. What about you?"

"Yuck. I could depress Mr. Chips with my war stories. Here, look what I found on my desk after lunch." Colleen opened her locker and felt around the upper shelf. She turned and she had a small foil packet in her hand. "Can you believe it?"

"What is it?"

Colleen held it closer and Rhea could see the word TROJAN in large blue letters.

"That's obscene!" Rhea said. But she felt her throat tighten and she had to strain to keep from laughing.

"That ain't exactly the word I'd have chosen. Oh, well . . ." And Colleen threw it back in her locker. "It might come in handy one of these days. Listen, what are you doing now? You want to come over for a drink? I'll play my new Linda Ronstadt for you."

"I'd love to, but I have an errand to run."

"Errands. I haven't paid my power bill for two months. I keep buying these stupid records."

"That drink sounds nice. If I get through in time I will come by."

"I'm sorry I ruined your party the other night."

"That was a week and a half ago and you didn't ruin it."

"I must have—I get so drunk."

"You *were* pretty high."

"I knew it."

"But you didn't ruin anything."

"Are you being nice?"

"No."

"Then I must be slipping. Thanks, kid. Drop by if you can." Then Colleen whispered, loudly: "Can you believe that fucking rubber?"

12

"You're leaving tomorrow," said Rhea.

"Tomorrow morning," said Kate.

"It will be a long exhausting trip."

"I get a lot of work done on planes. I find it relaxing, a good place to think."

"I just daydream," said Rhea.

Kate poured the tea. They were sitting in Loney's living room. It looked quite nice. Kate had moved the dining table to a corner. In the late afternoon shadows the room looked comfortable and even snug. Rhea glanced out the tall narrow window at the bright gray sky and she thought she could daydream easily in this room. She smelled something cooking in the oven, a roast perhaps, and she thought she had never been so warm and comfortable in this house. It had become a home.

"I couldn't let you get away," she began, "without talking—"

"Sugar?"

"No, thank you. I couldn't let you go away thinking that I didn't want to help Jim. . . ."

"I never gave it a thought."

Rhea sighed. "I hope you won't misunderstand. I know you wanted me to help you—to get him away from here. I know you wanted him to come to Washington with you."

"It's a little late. He won't. He has already informed me that he's happy right here."

"I don't think that's true. But I guess I knew he wouldn't go with you. I knew that from the beginning."

Kate looked at Rhea. She could have liked her. "And you did nothing to help. In a way, I can understand why you would want him to remain here. He is something of a toy. I understand that. But I can't believe you wouldn't want something better for him. You're going to leave, maybe not tomorrow, but soon, the end of the school year perhaps. You and I are going to go away to better things, but what about him? He'll still be here, in this house, drinking at that kitchen table and looking forward to nothing. I wanted—no—I needed your help. I thought I made that clear in my letter. I thought I conveyed a sense of urgency. I honestly thought you would help."

Rhea set her tea down. They were sitting side by side on the overstuffed couch, but Kate had turned away from her.

"I don't think you're being fair to me when you say I only want a toy. He's never been that to me. I know you've thought about him and his life a lot longer than I have, but I think we've both come to the conclusion that he is a human being. And we both love him and want what's best for him. Please don't think he's a toy to me." The soft steadiness in her voice surprised her. She hadn't expected herself to remain so calm. "You're right about me leaving Harlem, but it will be sooner than you think. I'm leaving right at the end of this term. And I want to take Jim with me."

Kate sat back on the couch and looked at Rhea. Her dark eyes narrowed and she couldn't help the mistrust that filled them. She had become used to dealing with people in terms of bluffs, of power plays and trade-offs, and she never took words at face value, as though they were meant. But as she looked at the small blond woman beside her, she wondered as she had upon arriving at the simplicity of this life. Yet a doubt persisted. "I hope you won't take this wrong, but it's been troubling me since we met—what exactly do you see in my brother? Besides his being a human being with potential? I can see that you are a woman of quality, and he is a man almost devoid of tangible qualities. I say this as his sister, as much as it hurts."

Rhea smiled. "I know it must seem strange. Sometimes it seems to me that we are the odd couple. We do come from completely different backgrounds. As you say, I have had advantages—more than I've taken advantage of, I'm afraid. But I came to Harlem to get away from all that and to find something. I wasn't at all proud of myself or my life. I had never really worked at anything. I'm twenty-nine and this was my first job. I thought coming up here would be a complete break with my past. It has been; not always pleasantly, I might add. I met Jim and I was just curious about him. No more. I found out who he was, that he had been a bright student, a basketball player, and I was intrigued. He was shy, yet charming, and he was totally different from any man I knew. The others were what you might expect in a city like Dallas—lawyer types, rich types, ambitious types. At first, with Jim, I thought it would be a—you'll hate me—a diversion, a chance to be frivolous." Rhea stopped for a moment and thought. "I guess you're right—in the beginning he was a toy. Not now. To get back to your question, I love him. For what he is and for what he might become. I would like to convince you that I'm not doing this out of any need for charity or social work. I'm doing it for myself, which I suppose raises another question."

Kate pressed her lips together. Then she stood and walked

to the window. She was wearing a black silk shirt, black slacks, and with her black hair, she looked almost like a shadow in the darkening room. She clasped her hands behind her and stood without saying anything. A light snow had begun to fall. Each flake fell clean and dry, and she thought about Washington winters, the grit of those wet winters. She had chosen them and she could live with them. Still, she envied this crisp snow and the way it covered everything with a feeling of permanence. She turned from the window. "I'm going to feel awful about this in the morning, but right now I believe you and I want what is best for him. I think you are." And she said, "Will you try to take him to Dallas with you?"

"Seattle. Don't ask me why I chose Seattle. I guess it just seems like a place to escape to."

"And do you think he will go with you?"

"I hope so. I mentioned the idea one night, in an oblique sort of way, and he seemed interested. At least, in Seattle. He said he had been in the army out there."

"That's right." Kate rubbed her upper arms. It was getting chilly. "He sent me some ivory polar bear salt and pepper shakers."

"He told me." Rhea stood and slipped into her coat. "He said they were lovely. He loves you very much."

"I still have them." Kate seemed distracted for a moment. Then she said, "I suppose he does, doesn't he?"

"You're very important to him."

"That's nice of you." Kate stepped toward Rhea and hugged her, perfunctorily. "I hope we get to know each other. I hope we get the opportunity."

"We will. I'm just sure of it."

"I'm sorry Jim wasn't here."

"I'm not."

"Will you stay for dinner?"

"I'd love to, but I have several things to do."

13

On the morning of the day Kate was to leave, she and Loney drove out to Snake Butte. It was early dawn and the sky to the east had started to turn a fresh pink. A thin snow on the raised road squealed beneath the tires of the rented car. Loney drove the rutted miles away from the dawn. And when they reached the butte he switched off the beams and crawled another quarter mile until they were opposite the small reservoir. He stopped the car but left the motor running.

"This is the last time," Kate said again, her voice as formal and dark as the suit she was wearing. "I will never come back here."

"We were close this time, except for—"

"I have a life of my own," Kate interrupted. "You are not a part of it anymore, by your own choosing. You have nothing left. Anything you do from now on you will do without conviction, without spirit. You reject me. You reject Rhea. You have nothing."

Loney leaned back and put his hands on his thighs and studied them. "I can't leave," he said, and he almost knew why. He thought of his earlier attempts to create a past, a background, an ancestry—something that would tell him who he was. Now he wondered if he had really tried. He had always admired Kate's ability to live in the present, but he had also wondered at her lack of need to understand her past. Maybe she had the right idea; maybe it was the present that mattered, only the present. But even as he thought this he saw the woman that Christmas Eve, his hand in her hair.

He looked out his window. The fissured gray walls of the butte were beginning to lighten and cast shadows. He didn't like the butte. Even as a kid, when he and Pretty Weasel and

Yellow Eyes rode out on Pretty Weasel's father's horses before dawn to fish, he had felt the dim walls watching him and he didn't like it. There were faces in the walls. He had discovered them then, and he saw them now. He had never looked closely because he didn't want to recognize any of the faces, and certainly not his own.

But there was one face that haunted him, and he knew the time was wrong, but this was to be his last chance to know.

"That woman," he said, not knowing, "that woman . . ." And he looked up at the gray walls changing into faces. "When you left the very first time, I stayed with her, she said she was our aunt and her name started with an S. I remember Christmas when she started crying and I put my hand in her hair. . . ." He wanted to say that she was the woman he had tried hardest to love, throughout the years, and now, but he saw the cruelty of it, and he said, "Where is she?"

And the car was empty of voices. Only the white whir of the car's heater broke the silence. The gray light fell across Kate's face and she thought, I am a failure even at this. I can't even pretend to be a good sister. And she thought that her love for her brother was that of a lover seeking a perfect love. She had not thought it before. Now she knew that she was crushed as a rejected lover might be. And she thought that somewhere in his cluttered mind, he knew it too.

The ice on the small reservoir was beginning to shine and when she looked up at the butte her eyes were dazzled by the streaks of yellow and she said, "Dead." Simply.

And he said, "Dead." He said it as though he were learning a new language. And then he said, "What was she?"

And Kate said, "She was your poor father's lover."

"She wasn't just a woman," Loney said.

"She and your father—"

"Our father."

"—were lovers for a good many years. When he left us that dark night, he left her too. You were ten. She—her name was

Sandra—took you in. You hadn't had a mother since you were a year old and she must have thought you needed looking after."

"What about you? Why didn't she take you in too? You were my sister."

Kate looked at the far foothills of the Bearpaws. In the dawn light they rose, a golden toast, against the gray of the western sky. From the warmth of the car they looked summery and she wished for summer and sweat and thirst.

"You were my sister," Loney said again.

"I wouldn't live with her."

"Didn't you like her?"

"I don't know."

Kate thought of the summers of their youth, the hot quiet days, the flies thick and slow against the screens. She thought of the small cottonwood in the backyard and the afternoons she had spent teaching him to read and write and add. She taught him the things she learned in school, and although he was five years younger than she, he picked much of it up. It had started out as a game, something to do to pass the summer afternoons, but soon she found herself obsessed with teaching him. Even in those days she thought of learning as a kind of salvation, a way to get up and out of being what they were, two half-breed kids caught in the slack water of a minor river.

Now as she sat in the car watching the sky lighten behind the Bearpaws, she thought it ironic that she was given the opportunity to teach her brother because they lived with a father who ignored them. It was only after he abandoned them. . .

"Why wouldn't you live with her?"

"I had a chance to go away—to go to a better place."

"A boarding school?"

"A better place. . ." But Kate had known back then that

she couldn't compete with Sandra, she didn't know how to compete with a woman. It was because Sandra was a good woman who loved them that she left. She had felt she would lose her brother and she couldn't take that. She had lost her mother and father, but neither of them meant much to her and so their separate leavings were bearable, even welcome. For a few exhilarating days after their father left, she thought that she would raise her brother herself. But then the agency people started coming around, and finally Sandra offered to take them in. Kate had seen her brother's reaction to Sandra and she knew that she would lose him. So she chose to go away herself. Now she wondered if that had been a mistake, whether if she had stayed with her brother things would be different now.

"How did she die?" Loney said.

"I don't remember—an accident, something. Don't you remember? You should," Kate said impatiently. "We'd better leave. I don't want to miss my plane."

But Loney sat for a moment. Strangely, he didn't remember. The two years with Sandra were like a dream. Kate lit a cigarette and rested her head on the back of the seat, exhaling the smoke as though she were emptying her body of air. A bird lifted from the cliffs of the butte and drove high into the sky. Loney watched it, the steady rhythm of its wings as it got smaller and smaller.

"Why haven't you married?" he said.

"I never met a man who could stand me."

"Do you ever think about your past—our past?"

"I gave it up a long time ago. We have no past. What's the point in thinking about it?"

"I don't know." Loney leaned forward and put the car in gear. "No point really." He turned the car around and headed it toward the main highway. He pulled the visor down against the sun. "I love you," he said, and he felt oddly cheerful.

14

There was something determined about Harlem as it readied itself for the Christmas season. Except for a few decorations—a red cellophane wreath with an electric candle in the Coast-to-Coast store, children's cutouts of snowflakes in the laundromat window, and a cardboard Santa pointing out Buttrey's holiday items (hard candy 59¢, tinsel 29¢, hot buttered rum batter 89¢)—and the fact that the stores stayed open until nine every evening, it was hard to tell that a season of joy had visited itself on the community. But the weekly *Harlem News* proclaimed the event with a notation beside the weather box: "Only 12 More Shopping Days Till Christmas, Joyeux Noel." And there were kids on the streets.

Kenny Hart was shaking Christmas trees in the Lions Club lot beside the Texaco station. He had read somewhere that if you could shake the needles loose, then that tree was too dry. And so he strolled through the lot, shaking needles off the trees.

"Don't damage the merchandise, Kenny," said a dry little man in a red plaid Scotch cap.

"You bastards have got it sewed up, don't you?"

The little man laughed. He was tickled. "There ain't another tree lot in forty miles—least none where you'll get trees as good as these."

"If I served drinks as bad as these trees, they'd have my license within the hour. My balls. No, listen, c'mere. . ."

The little man sidled up to Kenny. He was already laughing. He knew what was coming.

Kenny leaned down. "How many North Dakotans does it take to eat a rabbit?"

The little man shook his head and laughed. He pulled his

ear flap up. He knew it was going to be a good one.

"Give it a try, Harold."

But the little man shook his head. He had heard it before but he couldn't remember the answer.

"Two. One to watch for cars."

Harold said, "Ah, ah, ah." He slapped himself on the side of the head and said, "Ah, ah, ah." Then he said, "I'll have to remember that one. That ain't too shabby."

Kenny held up a tree. "I'll give you two bucks for this one."

"Oh, no you don't." And Harold grew shrewd. "That's one of our six-footers. One dollar a foot."

"But look at all these goddamned needles on the ground," Kenny protested.

"That one there came all the way from the Rocky Mountains. That one there's one of our favorites."

Kenny talked the little man down a foot, gave him a five and threw the tree into the back of his pickup. He loved Christmas. He drove down to Kennedy's, listening to Bing Crosby on the radio.

Business was good this evening and that was one of the things Kenny loved about Christmas. It was good for business and he made a lot of money. But he loved even more to see his bar filled. It always reminded him of the way he had envisioned his bar when he bought it back in '59. A bar full of good people having themselves a real good time. And he recognized most of them—a couple of ranchers, several townies and a bunch from the agency. He noticed a group of white people sitting at a table near the jukebox. He hadn't seen them before, but he figured them to be schoolteachers or maybe BIA people from the area office down in Billings. Christmas made for strange barfellows.

George LaMere was tending bar.

"Georgie, gimme a hot one, huh?" Kenny said and watched him turn to fix the drink. LaMere was the quietest man Kenny had ever known. It had taken the better part of a year for

Kenny to learn that LaMere had spent fifteen years down in Deer Lodge for killing a woman. He never did find out where this had happened or why. All Kenny knew was that LaMere hadn't done anything wrong in the two years he had worked for him. He had no complaints about LaMere.

"Georgie, c'mere."

Kenny watched him bring the hot whiskey. One thing was certain—LaMere was imperturbable. He worked around liquor with the stoicism of a recovered alcoholic. And Kenny was certain he was just that.

"Buy those white folks a drink. Over there. No, wait. Wait a minute. Buy everyone a drink." As LaMere turned, Kenny whispered after him, "Don't tell them who it's on. No, say 'On the house.' "

Kenny looked around. He figured he would set the tree up after the bar closed tonight. He usually set it up in the corner on the other side of the jukebox, but it never seemed the right place. He wanted it to be the first thing people noticed when they came through the door. Maybe back by that partition that sheltered the pool table. They ought to let kids in bars on Christmas. Kenny had had two wives but no kids. He always regretted that. He could have had grandchildren by now, a whole houseful of kids. Jesus Christ, they'd be just right, full of piss and vinegar.

"Hey, Kenny!"

It was Ike. He was sitting with a young Indian halfway down the bar. His thin white shirt made him look even scrawnier than he was.

"What the hell was the name of that woman in here the other night?"

"Carloada," said Kenny.

Ike turned to his partner and winked. "Carloada?" he said.

"Carloada Shit," Kenny called. "I hear she's looking for you."

The two ranchers at the bar turned to Kenny and laughed.

Goddamn that Ike, Kenny thought, always earning a drink. And goddamn me for being a sucker.

15

Pretty Weasel was waiting for Loney when he stepped out of the liquor store. Loney knew it when he saw him, but Pretty Weasel had his Scotch cap pulled down over his eyes. He was leaning against the wall of Merle's Confectionery. For an instant Loney thought of dashing up the street the other way. He used to be able to outrun Pretty Weasel in high school. But he could think of no graceful way. He started to walk by Pretty Weasel.

"Same time, same place."

Loney turned.

"I saw you here last week. Same time, same place."

Loney clutched his wine. "I'm not very original."

Pretty Weasel laughed and pushed himself away from the wall. "Long time, no see," he said. "Where have you been, my friend?"

Loney gestured helplessly at the street with his free hand.

"I'm going hunting tomorrow. Pheasant. Down by Strike's."

Loney knew the place. He knew what Pretty Weasel was talking about. They had hunted there as kids, in high school, Pretty Weasel with his twelve-gauge and Loney with his single-shot .22. The grainfields down there were thick with pheasants, even in winter, if the winter wasn't bad, if the snow had blown or melted off. Loney hadn't thought of those days in years, but now the sudden vision of them bumping across the fields in Pretty Weasel's father's pickup, slamming on the brakes when the pheasants scrambled to the ditches and the dry slough, the thick blast of the twelve-gauge, followed by another, and another, made Loney's head light with unquiet memories.

"You want me to come get you?"

Loney held his bottle close to his chest. One on the fly and two on the ground. Two on the fly. Once all three on the fly.

Loney remembered his frustration as he squeezed off his single shot at a running cock, then the whir of his wings as Loney struggled to reload. Once he even carried his shells in his mouth so he wouldn't have to dig in a pocket, but his tongue turned gray and he thought he had lead poisoning.

"We'll have a drink. We'll talk about it."

Then it was dark and Pretty Weasel led the way across the street to Kennedy's. He had been six feet two in high school, but he looked taller than that now. In his down vest he looked dark and massive. Loney glanced away at the hardware store and he saw the red cellophane wreath with its electric candle in the window. "Christmas," he said, as though he had just thought of it.

"That's right, son—Christmas." And Pretty Weasel waited and put his arm around Loney's shoulder and laughed.

16

Colleen was drinking the tequilas almost as fast as the bartender could bring them. She had no drinking buddies in Harlem and so she usually drank at home alone. The few times she had been out on her own she had got into terrible messes, the kind that took days to recover from, physically and emotionally. But this—this was just like college all over again, except there wasn't any lemon and salt. She felt reckless; she had already called Rhea a pussy—"Don't be such a pussy"—when Rhea declined a shot of tequila. Rhea had given her a disgusted look, but the three men loved it because they felt reckless too. They had driven fifty miles to feel reckless, all the way from Havre. Two of them taught in the high school there and the third was a student at the college. The two teachers had met Colleen at a convention down in Great Falls a couple of months earlier and she had promised to line them up if they ever got to Harlem. So she had talked Rhea into it. She hadn't counted on the college student and she couldn't find him a date. She and Rhea were the only single women she knew in Harlem.

"Do yourself a favor," she murmured in Rhea's direction.

"I'm having a ball," Rhea said. "An absolute ball."

Colleen knew she was going to be shitty. "All right, Miss Puss," she said.

"If you call me that again I'll leave."

"What part of the South you from?" said the college student. He had a lazy attractiveness about him with his lean, almost pretty face and long sandy hair parted in the middle. He was eating peanuts off the table.

"Dallas. Texas."

"I love the way you say 'Dallas.' We don't get many Southern belles around this part of the country. What brought you all the way up here?" He had a small red pimple just below his left nostril.

"A mistake, a dreadful mistake."

The college student chuckled. He had been aware of the pimple all day. He turned to one of the teachers and said, "Your turn, Herbert."

But Rhea had turned her attention to the two men who had just walked in the door. She didn't recognize the first one. The second was Loney.

It had been a week since Kate left and in that week Rhea had lost all her confidence. She had seen Loney twice, early on, and she had mentioned Seattle twice and each time Loney had gone blank, as though he had never been to Seattle, as though Seattle had no importance to him. She hadn't asked him point-blank if he wanted to go to Seattle with her because she didn't want to be hurt point-blank. And so this past week, for the first time since coming to Harlem, she had felt absolutely alone.

And now she felt awkward. She couldn't just sit there and she couldn't walk up to him and say, "Well, Mr. Loney, this is a coincidence." She was confused and she felt that she didn't know him, had never known him. And she felt a kind of anger work its way up through her confusion.

"Oh, God," said Colleen. "Oh, my God," she said, for she had seen Pretty Weasel and hated him even worse than Loney. He had been one of her early bad experiences.

Kenny stood at the far end of the bar, drinking his hot whiskey and watching the women's reactions to Loney and Pretty Weasel. He didn't quite know what was going on, but it wasn't pleasant, especially with the dark-haired one. He figured she was liable to get mean. She was drunk enough. And she had those white boys with her. Kenny had developed an eye for trouble and he saw the potential now. And he wasn't about to allow a racial incident to happen in his bar. He knew he was overreacting—things like this happened rarely—but he also knew Pretty Weasel could be violent when disturbed. Five or six years back, Kenny had watched him punch out a couple of Malta boys at a football game. It was quick but brutal.

And then there was the business of Loney senior and Loney junior. They hadn't become aware of each other yet, but they would. Ike was such a miserable old fart that he might start badgering his son just for the sport in it. Ike was harmless, but Kenny wasn't sure about his son. He had never been sure of Jim Loney. He was not geared for survival like his old man. He had gotten along so far, but Kenny felt in his guts that Jim Loney would go off someday. If he were pressed, he could only offer, "I've seen it in his eyes." But he would never be pressed because a man like Loney just wasn't that important to anyone.

Kenny walked around the counter and tied on his apron. He felt he could handle things better from there. George La-

Mere was staring at him from the other end of the bar. Kenny wasn't due to start his shift for another hour and a half. "Take a break, Georgie," he called. LaMere finished wiping the bar, then sat down on the end stool, his eyes never leaving Kenny.

"What do you say, gentlemen?"

"Couple of Luckys," said Pretty Weasel.

"Merry Christmas," said Loney.

"That's the spirit. Merry Christmas. Hey." Kenny leaned over the bar. "What's the state bird of North Dakota?"

Pretty Weasel dropped a couple of dollars on the counter.

"The housefly," Kenny said.

The two ranchers laughed. They were from up north.

Ike craned his neck and looked around the ranchers to see who Kenny was talking to. He saw Pretty Weasel's chest and he saw his son's thin face. In a way it was his own face: the profile that he had never seen, the identical slightly large ear, the horizontal jaw line and the dark eye set back a ways from the straight nose. He had his mother's hair, Ike thought, black, almost blue. And her dark skin.

He tried not to think about his wife because it did no good. He didn't hold her leaving him against her anymore because that, too, did no good. But he didn't like the fact that he and his son lived in the same town. Her son was always there to remind him of Eletra and a part of his past that he had walked away from. If he held anything against his wife it was the fact that she had left first. She had beaten him to it. So he was left with two kids and no desire to be a father. But he had stuck with them for ten years, off and on, until Kate was sixteen or seventeen. She was taking care of her younger brother by then, so he didn't feel bad when he caught a ride up to Havre one night after the bars closed. After a year of bumming around, he worked his way down to Great Falls, and then to Butte, where he put in eleven years in the Mountain Con mine, working for the Company. He enjoyed the money and the women and he once drank all night with Evel Knievel before he became famous and an asshole. Then it ended when a crawl space between tunnels collapsed on him and crushed three vertebrae. When he got out of the hospital, he settled up with the Company and moved back to Harlem. The settlement was long gone but he did get a monthly disability check and he could live on that, most of the time in peace. Except for those unavoidable times when he saw his son, who reminded him of Eletra. It didn't occur to him to feel guilty for abandoning his children.

He settled back on his stool. Be cool, he thought, cool as a cucumber. This is still your town. You own it. And he turned to the young Indian beside him. "You're a good man, Willard. I knew your father, and his father, and his father's father. You're the last of a long line of good men."

"What do you mean, 'last'?"

"Hell, you know as well as I do you're going to marry one of these goddamn white women and that'll be the last of that pure strain. You're as good as a white man already. Or as bad."

Willard turned around on his stool and looked at the white women behind him and thought about this.

The college student looked up at Willard and followed his gaze down to Rhea. Fucking Indian, he thought, fucking pimple. He had gone back to the bathroom to squeeze it and now it was bleeding. He dabbed at it with his handkerchief. He hated Kennedy's and he couldn't believe that a woman like Rhea lived in this town. She was something else. But so was he. Not like these turkeys he'd come down with. He figured if he could get her away from there, alone, she would see that. He was fascinated by her, not because she was good-looking (she was that), but because she was different—Southern, older and aloof. He decided he liked these qualities. And he was determined to strip them away.

He crossed his legs and looked at her breasts and small, almost sloping shoulders. She was vulnerable and he thought of her large white teeth.

17

"You don't talk much anymore. Used to be we couldn't shut you up. What the hell's the matter with you?"

"Cat's got my tongue."

"Well, something's sure funny here. When I saw you coming out of the liquor store, I thought, Hey, what the hell's going on, me and Loney used to be the best of friends, he used to be the best friend I ever had. . . ." Pretty Weasel shook a cigarette out of Loney's pack.

"Times have changed," Loney said and he said it deliberately, for his own benefit. He felt small beside Pretty Weasel, as though they had been growing physically apart, he smaller, Pretty Weasel bigger.

"We can remedy that in a damn hurry."

"Yes," said Loney and he almost laughed.

Pretty Weasel lit the cigarette from Loney's and watched the smoke go away from him. He didn't smoke, ever, but he thought of the cigarette as a kind of offering. "I'm in with the old man. You knew that, didn't you?" He would start with this.

And Loney said, "That's what you came back for."

"Naw—you think that? I'll tell you why I came back—because I couldn't stand those people down there. You know why. Because they put the pressure on me, all this Indian bullshit. You know what they called me in the newspaper? Super Chief."

"That's what we used to call you."

"That was different. Up here it didn't mean anything."

"What did it mean down there?"

"Indian play basketball good, Indian friend of the white man. I don't mean maybe, either."

Loney thought about this. In the service they had called

him Chief and he was only half Indian. It always startled Loney that when he stepped out of his day-to-day existence he was considered an Indian. He never felt Indian. Indians were people like the Cross Guns, the Old Chiefs—Amos After Buffalo. They lived an Indian way, at least tried. When Loney thought of Indians, he thought of the reservation families, all living under one roof, the old ones passing down the wisdom of their years, of their family's years, of their tribe's years, and the young ones soaking up their history, their places in their history, with a wisdom that went beyond age.

He remembered when the Cross Guns family used to come to town. The car would be full of adults and kids, and when they scattered to their various appointments, only old Emil Cross Guns would be left, sitting in the back seat in his black suit coat and black hat, black neckerchief knotted around his ropy old neck. Loney recalled going up to the window and touching his hand and the old man saying something in Gros Ventre. All the kids used to touch his hand because he was a medicine man. It was Pretty Weasel who had told Loney that Emil had cured his older sister of infantile paralysis.

Emil was dead now and those days were gone to Loney. Everything was changed and the old ones did not exist. Even Pretty Weasel came from a different kind of family. Both his father and his mother had gone to college, back in the days when Indians didn't go to college. And his father had been tribal chairman for a number of years. There was a picture in their house of him shaking hands with President Eisenhower. Now he was old, but in a white man way, thrown away. Not like Emil Cross Guns.

Loney thought this and he grew sad, not for Pretty Weasel's father, nor for Emil Cross Guns, but for himself. He had no family and he wasn't Indian or white. He remembered the day he and Rhea had driven out to the Little Rockies. She had said he was lucky to have two sets of ancestors. In truth he had none.

"Pheasant, my man," said Pretty Weasel. "We're going after those wily ones tomorrow."

Loney looked up and beyond Pretty Weasel and was astonished to see Rhea hurry by him.

18

Once outside, Rhea ran the half block to her car. The stores were still open but the street was virtually deserted. She ran and the air was cold and she felt her eyes fill with tears. For a brief practical moment she felt that she should have said goodbye, but to whom? This is crazy, she thought, and she started her car and backed out into the street. She put the car into forward gear and it jumped forward, then stalled. "Damn you," she said. "Damn you." She glanced toward Kennedy's and she saw a figure standing in the light. At first she thought it was the college boy, but when the figure stepped off the curb and walked toward the car, she recognized Loney. She wiped the tears from the corners of her eyes with a gloved hand.

She rolled down her window and said, "Hello." Then she said, "Get in." She said it almost coyly and the anger returned. She didn't need to be coy anymore.

Loney walked around the car and got in. He seemed wary and he closed and locked the door behind him as if to shut out a threatening crowd. But the street was virtually deserted as Rhea started the car and put it in gear. Neither of them looked in the store windows and she felt as though they were the only souls out in Harlem. She drove past her street and then past his street and soon they were on the outskirts of town where the main street met the new highway. Rhea turned left onto the highway and drove slowly toward the agency and the reservation. She didn't know what else to do.

Finally she said, "What is it that troubles you?"

Loney looked down at his hands and he discovered that he still had the bottle of wine in the paper sack. Without thinking, he twisted the top and he heard the paper tear and the metal cap break free. "I've been bad to you," he said. "Partly that—I've been very bad to you." He tightened the cap and he looked out the window and saw the lights of the agency twinkling through the dark cottonwoods along the Milk River. "I think you should never have met me." The fields were covered with an old snow.

"But what is it that really troubles you? For pity's sake, don't you know I want to help you?"

"It's not something . . . I don't even know myself. It has to do with the past." But Loney realized this wasn't good enough. He had thought and said it too often to believe it anymore. "It has to do with certain things. I know it has to do with my mother and father, but there are other things. It has to do with an aunt I lived with when I was a kid. I loved her and she died. That's okay. It was enough to love her. But I would like to know who she really was and how she died and why. I don't know."

Rhea felt her hands loosen on the steering wheel. She hadn't realized how tense she had been. But Loney was talking finally and she held her breath, in her mind urging him on.

"I know this is kind of strange, but I see a bird—I don't know what kind of bird it is—but I see it every night. Sometimes it flies slowly enough so that I can almost study it, but even then . . . it is a bird I've never seen in real life. I don't know. It comes and I look at it and then it fades away."

"Is it a dream?"

"It comes when I'm awake, but late at night when I'm tired—or drunk." Loney was silent for a moment. Then he said, "I don't know what this has to do with anything, certainly it has nothing to do with my aunt. It just comes every night, and every night I think, This must have some meaning. Sometimes I think it is a vision sent by my mother's people. I must interpret it, but I don't know how."

Loney paused again, then sighed. "There is a Bible phrase. It's crazy. It popped into my mind a couple of months ago at a football game. 'Turn away from man in whose nostrils is breath, for of what account is he?' I haven't looked it up because I'm afraid I will find it and it will be bad."

"It's from Isaiah," said Rhea.

Loney looked at her. "I think of it quite a bit. It just pops into my mind and I don't know how I know it. I went to a Catholic boarding school, and then I lived in a minister's house—it must come from one or the other. The minister was kind of a screwball. Maybe he put it in my mind. The point is, it's there and it bothers me. I want to make a little sense out of my life and all I get are crazy visions and Bible phrases. They're like puzzles."

By now they were almost to the bridge that spanned the Milk River. A few hundred yards beyond stood the entrance to the agency. Rhea had never actually been to the agency, but she knew there was a hospital back in there, along with some office buildings and a community of government houses. One of her best students, Arlene Small, lived out here with her mother. Arlene, like most of her Indian students, was shy, and Rhea had often wished she could take the girl home with her, to get to know her, but there were barriers. There were always barriers, some artificial, some natural.

She heard the tires hum as they crossed the bridge and she heard herself say, "You have decided not to come to Seattle."

"I can't. Not yet."

And Rhea heard herself again: "Did it ever occur to you that if you left you would leave these . . . visions behind? You might become so involved with a new life that your past would fade away—that bird would fade away for good."

"I don't know that I want that to happen."

Rhea slowed the car and turned off at the entrance to the agency. She held her wrist close to the illuminated dash panel. Her watch said 8:30. It felt more like midnight. She drove the lane back into the agency and as she neared the hospital, she said, "I'm going home first. I'll gather myself together, then I'll make a decision." She watched a dog trot past them on the other side of the road. Its tongue was hanging out and it ignored them. Rhea said, "What did you offer me? No, I'm talking to myself. What did you offer me?" She turned right at the hospital, toward some buildings. There was a moon, a half moon, and it struck the snow and the white buildings and Rhea could see the small rectangular houses beyond. "I think you offered me love. Is that correct? Not an all-consuming love, by any means, but a love I wasn't familiar with, without obligation, without pretense. An unpretentious love. A year's worth. More than I deserved, less than fulfilling. But love."

Loney wasn't used to that word. He said, "Yes," but he looked out his window.

Rhea looked past him and they were in the small housing project. Most of the picture windows were bare, without curtains, without lamps or light. But a couple had Christmas trees in them; the blues and reds and yellows of their ornaments and lights seemed festive and otherworldly. She wondered vaguely which house Arlene Small lived in. "It's almost Christmas," she said softly. And she thought, Why am I off the track? What is there about us that puts me off the track so easily? And she said, "We're finished. . . ."

"It would be for the best."

"It seems so simple."

"It's not."

"No, of course not. This is your country, isn't it? It means a great deal to you."

Loney thought for a moment. "I've never understood it. Once

in a while I look around and I see things familiar and I think I will die here. It's my country then. Other times I want to leave, to see other things, to meet people, to die elsewhere."

"Why must you think of it in terms of dying?" Rhea turned the car around the small square. "Is it just a matter of dying? Don't you want other things? It seems so limiting."

For the first time in a long time Loney laughed. "I'm sorry," he said. "I'm sorry."

"Don't be. Please laugh some more. It sounds so good after so long. It was a dumb thing to say, wasn't it?"

"I wish it was. It wasn't, though. Dying *is* limiting. Thinking about it is even more so, in a way."

"I hate to think of me leaving and you thinking about dying. It seems so pointless, our having been together."

"I won't think of it anymore." Loney looked at Rhea in the half light of the moonlit car. "It was the wrong thing. I don't want you to go, but I don't have enough in me to make you want to stay."

The hospital was dark brick and serene and Rhea turned again onto the lane that led to the entrance to the agency. "I won't stay," she said. The moonlight got brighter off the snow and she said, "I will not stay here." She felt dry inside and she said, "Nothing can make me stay here without you."

19

Loney couldn't sleep because if he slept he would dream, so he stared into the blackness of the small bedroom. From time to time he would roll over onto his side and grope for the bottle of wine beside the bed. He tried to think of nothing, but many thoughts came out of the dark and left him bewildered. He thought he had not blinked in a long time and so he blinked. He thought he heard Swipesy moan in the kitchen but the dog had been dead since Thanksgiving. And he thought it strange that he hadn't missed Swipesy at all, and yet he never thought of him as being dead. Just as he didn't think of Sandra as being dead. Or Kate as being gone for good. Or Rhea as leaving for good. He had wiped the slate clean, but it didn't occur to him.

He lay in bed and dreaded dawn. Pretty Weasel would come to take him hunting and he had no desire to hunt or to see Pretty Weasel. And he thought, After tomorrow I will have no future. Everybody and everything will be gone out of my life. Kate was right—I have nothing left, no conviction, no spirit. After tomorrow's slim purpose I will simply exist.

He lit another cigarette and smoked for a moment without thinking. Suddenly an image of his father as a younger man drifted into his mind. He saw the slick hair and the slightly too large ears and the white shirt. He was carrying a shotgun and Loney recognized it as his father's sixteen-gauge. He carried it against his chest as though he were posing for a picture and Loney remembered that picture from out of his past. Then the vision Loney had had a month before exploded in the darkness and his father was covered with snow and ice and he was grinning as he pressed the gun into Loney's hands.

Loney sat up and swung his legs off the bed. He was sweating and he felt sick. His father was still here. He was the last one left to Loney.

He hurried into the kitchen, across the cold linoleum, and switched on the light above the sink. He looked at the clock beside the refrigerator. Three thirty-five. Swipesy growled and Loney whirled around, but there was no dog.

He turned on the lamp on the kitchen table and then he looked out the window and he saw his father grinning in at him. He wasn't covered with snow and ice, but his face was blue.

Loney opened his mouth. Then he motioned for his father to come in, but his father only grinned. "Get out of here, you sonofabitch!" he yelled. And his father moved back into the darkness. Loney ran outside and stood at the corner of the house. He looked toward the street but he saw no movement. He saw nothing until he looked toward his window and he saw the large flakes falling against the yellow light. His feet began to burn and he realized he was barefoot.

Three or four inches of new snow lay on the frozen ground. As his eyes adjusted, Loney found that it was not dark; the snow had lit the night to a dull clear gray. He looked out into the backyard toward the garage and he saw Swipesy sniffling the base of a cottonwood tree. He whistled and the dog looked up. For an instant it seemed to recognize Loney. Then it took off, disappearing beyond the garage.

"No pheasant today!" Loney called after the dog.

Back in his bedroom, he dressed himself. As he pulled the warm socks over his burning feet he wondered why Pretty Weasel would want to hunt together after all these years. When Pretty Weasel first suggested it, Loney thought it must be a test. But a test of what? Guts? Ability? It didn't make sense. Pretty Weasel had the drop on him in both departments. Friendship? How could that be? Pretty Weasel didn't need friends. Loney reached for his wine and his eyes got wet. A kind of hopelessness burned through the early morning hangover. He was hung over most of the time now. It had nothing to do with headaches and bad stomach. It was more a general numbness and a general forgetfulness of all but the most whimsical detail, the most random thought. Now he thought of the day Pretty Weasel went away to college. Loney and George Yellow Eyes had driven him to Billings to catch the plane to the University of Wyoming. They missed his plane because they were two days late. They had spent the days in Lewistown with some girls they had met during the state tournament the winter before. Later, at the airport, Pretty Weasel had said to Loney, "You should be going to college instead of me."

Then he said, "You're my best friend," and Loney and Yellow Eyes watched him get on the plane to Laramie.

20

Myron Pretty Weasel walked around to the back of Loney's small asbestos-brick house. Although it was still snowing a little, there was a hint of yellow on the eastern horizon. Pretty Weasel didn't drink much anymore and the five or six beers he had had with Loney the night before had thickened his mind. He didn't like that. Mornings were his best time and he didn't like his mind to be fucked up.

He pounded on the back door, his leather mittens muffling the noise in the false dawn. Then he pushed the door open and he saw Loney leaning over the table, his head raised as though he had just woken up. And he heard Loney say, "But it's snowing." And as he stepped into the kitchen he smelled the faint sourness of a man who lives alone.

"I've changed our plans," he said, glancing around the wreck of the kitchen. He walked to the sink and turned on the water. The fact that the tap worked seemed to interest him. "You got any coffee?"

"Not made."

"Then I'll make some. Where is it?"

Loney pointed to a cupboard to the left of the sink. Pretty Weasel opened it and took out a jar. "Instant," he said.

"Flavor crystals," said Loney.

Pretty Weasel found on the stove a saucepan that had never been scoured. The mineral deposits on the bottom resembled a satellite picture of the moon. But it looked faintly sanitary.

As he waited for the water to boil, he rinsed two cups and

set them on the table. He looked at Loney and was about to ask for sugar, but Loney shook his head.

Pretty Weasel walked through the hallway to the front of the house. To his surprise, the living room was orderly and clean. The furniture was tawdry, but there were pictures on the walls and curtains on the windows. There was a photograph in a gold frame on a knickknack shelf in one corner of the room. Pretty Weasel studied it in the light from the hallway. Although he had never seen her grown up, he figured it must be Kate. She was a beautiful woman, but she had been a beautiful, if skinny, girl. He looked around the room again and decided that Loney was a kitchen drunk.

As he poured the coffee he said, "We're going after deer. Get us a couple of those whitetails down by McFarland's. The snow's perfect."

"Why don't we hunt at your place?"

"No sport."

"Are you feeding them?"

"My private stock."

"I don't have a gun."

"I've got two. You can use my old thirty-thirty. I brought it."

"Get yourself a glass," Loney said, nodding toward the wine bottle.

"You always were a horse's ass. Have you had anything to eat? No, you wouldn't have. We'll drive into Dodson when we're done and eat lunch at Irene's." He circled the kitchen. "What the hell am I looking for?" Then he said, "What's Kate up to these days?"

"She's a big shot—education—in Washington, D.C. She was back here a couple of weeks ago. She asked about you."

"I doubt that." Pretty Weasel found a glass in the cupboard over the sink and poured himself some wine. He had had a crush on her as a boy, even though she was five years older. She was cold to him. She was cold to all of Loney's friends. They called her Ice Woman. She couldn't have been more than fifteen at the time. He hadn't seen her since. "I doubt it very much."

Loney said, "Shithead."

Pretty Weasel took a swallow of wine, then grimaced. "This stuff is real bad for you. Are you aware of that?"

"How do you propose to get to McFarland's?"

"We'll cross the river from the reservation side."

"But it's not frozen."

"Where have you been? Besides pickling your fucking brain with this stuff."

"Where have *you* been?" said Loney, and he was serious.

Pretty Weasel laughed suddenly and loudly. In the yellow kitchen the laughter seemed disjointed, as out of place as Loney's soundless bird. He laughed again, this time the bird turning gray in the chill beyond the walls.

"Where *have* you been?"

"Staying away from you juicers. Don't worry about it."

And in the next quiet seconds Loney realized that Pretty Weasel had come back only for this hunt. He had left the sad same life of Harlem, but he didn't know that Loney had left it too. They had gone opposite directions, Pretty Weasel to his father's ranch, Loney to his life of more absolute isolation. And now they were to hunt together.

For those seconds Loney felt a sense of knowledge without knowing what he had learned. Or the worth of it. Then it was gone.

21

The sun broke over the eastern horizon and they were riding in Pretty Weasel's new pickup. In the gun rack behind them a 30–06 and an old Winchester 30–30 filled the cab with the smell of oil.

"Dirty bastard," said Pretty Weasel, and he meant the sun. They were late.

Loney felt nothing but the warmth of the wine and a mild regard for the country they passed. It was a shallow country, filled with hayfields, thickets, stands of willow, and leafless cottonwoods that marked the course of a river without movement.

"We won it all once—remember that?" Pretty Weasel said this without passion.

They drove on in silence. Once Loney passed the bottle to Pretty Weasel and he took it, held it for a moment, then passed it back. "Fucking Yellow Eyes," he said, again without passion.

Loney was watching the river in his mind, the loops and bends as gracefully etched in the winter cover as a blue racer snake frozen in the grass. Loney always wondered how that river knew where to bend, why it wandered with such feckless purpose. He wondered if it always sought the lowest ground, or was his mind such a shambles that he assumed there was a reason behind its constant shifting? From the highway it looked aimless and vaguely malevolent and Loney thought there was something of that river in his own life and he didn't think about it.

By now the sun was well up over the horizon and they were still twenty minutes from McFarland's. They passed the pink church of Loney's dream and he glanced back through the rear window and saw a scaffolding with a large bell on top. It hadn't been in his dream.

"Boy, that fucking Yellow Eyes."

"What about that fucking Yellow Eyes?" said Loney.

"Well, don't you remember—how he almost blew it? Nine seconds? For Christ's sake?"

"He played a good game."

"Good game, he says. How many shots did he take—thirty, forty?"

"He made a lot of them," said Loney, gradually realizing

that he was thinking about Yellow Eyes for the first time in years.

"How about that last shot from half court. Nine seconds. He could have worked it down. He just choked."

"Well, all's well that end's well. You tipped it in and saved our ass. You ought to be grateful. That's probably what got you that scholarship to Wyoming."

"I'm grateful enough to bust *his* ass the next time I see him."

Loney was a little surprised that they were talking about that game. It had been the championship game, but it was only a speck of history now. And he was surprised and annoyed that it should be so important to Pretty Weasel.

"He was a glory hound, no two ways about it."

"He's dead," said Loney.

Pretty Weasel swung his head as slowly and deliberately as a cow in open country. "How?" he said.

"I don't know—some war."

"What war?"

"I don't know. Spanish-American maybe."

Pretty Weasel fixed his eyes on the road ahead of them and drove for several minutes. Then he said. "I'm sorry to hear that."

Loney took a small sip of wine. He was starting to feel good.

"What war was that?" Pretty Weasel's voice was small and low.

Loney laughed. He looked out the window at the rising sun. He shook his head as though to clear his mind, but the laughter came from an old source, another time, when he was always one jump ahead of Pretty Weasel, Yellow Eyes, all of them.

"You fucker," said Pretty Weasel. "You horse's ass."

Loney laughed and Pretty Weasel joined him. He hit Loney on the arm and grabbed the wine away from him. "You bastard." He laughed, and they both laughed, and the pickup jerked as Pretty Weasel made a grab for Loney's nuts.

Loney retrieved the bottle and took a good swallow. As he

screwed the cap down, he said, "He *is* dead." He felt almost human.

22

Pretty Weasel stood beside the pickup with his head lowered. Loney on the other side thought he was taking a leak. Then Pretty Weasel made a sign of the cross, just like in high school before he shot a free throw.

And then they were down beside the Milk River, looking at the shiny skin of ice.

"Wait," said Pretty Weasel. He slung the 30–06 across his back, got down on his belly and began to slither across. The ice was heaved up on the edges, slanting down toward the center. In the middle a shallow layer of slush glistened dully. Pretty Weasel got up on his hands and toes as though he were preparing to do a few push-ups, but he moved forward, one hand at a time, pulling his body over the slush. Then he dropped to his belly and continued his slow crawl until he stood up on the other side.

"Okay," he murmured.

"What am I going to do with this gun?" The 30–30 had no sling.

"Tuck it up under your coat." He sounded disgusted. "Make sure it's unloaded. I put some shells in this morning."

Loney levered the shells out, then shoved the rifle in the front of his parka. He got down on his hands and knees and looked across to Pretty Weasel. The distance seemed farther from this position. He was about to get up, but Pretty Weasel motioned him across with an impatient swing of his arm.

The ice was thick on the edge, but as Loney approached the center, he could see the water and the air bubbles. It seemed as though he were sliding across a mud puddle on a pane of morning ice. The water didn't look to be moving and yet the air bubbles moved off to his right, downstream. He got up on his hands and toes and started to pull himself across the slush. It had looked easy but it wasn't. He couldn't get a grip with his toes. Then the gun began to slide from his parka. He tried to walk on his hands, but his toes kept slipping. The butt of the rifle was dragging in the slush. He heard Pretty Weasel curse, so he lifted his left hand to shove the gun back up and he went down, his cheek striking the grainy slush. He got to his hands and knees almost as fast as he went down and he crawled the rest of the way at a fast amble.

"You all right?" Pretty Weasel was sitting on a windfall cottonwood, laughing and trying to appear concerned. "You looked like a porcupine."

Loney wiped his cheek with his coat sleeve and swore.

"Well, you'd better load up. No telling what's going to happen from here on out." Pretty Weasel giggled and turned and walked back into the trees and brush that grew along the river.

After a few minutes of trotting a cattle trail, they came upon the fields. They lay down behind a clump of teasels and scanned the cut-over wheat stubble. Pretty Weasel was intent as he squinted through his scope. Loney's eyes began to water from the sun's glare on the snow, so he looked beyond the fields to the prairies. Thirty miles to the north lay Canada. It occurred to him that he had never been to Canada. Once in high school they had scheduled a game with a Canadian town. They had joked all that week about whether the Canucks knew what a basketball was, but they didn't get to make the trip. The road north out of Harlem had been drifted shut. As Loney looked at the prairies he thought of the name of that town—Val Marie. It still sounded so foreign that he couldn't help wishing, even now, that they had made the trip.

"Remember that time we were going to play those Canucks?"

"Shhh. Over there."

And Loney followed Pretty Weasel's sightline to a stand of cattails that marked a slough two hundred yards away. A thick dark animal stood at the edge, its nose high in the air. It dropped to all fours and moved its head up and down rapidly. It seemed disoriented, perhaps blinded by the sun-struck field.

"Oh, yes," said Pretty Weasel. "I believe it is. I believe it is what I think it is."

They watched for a few more seconds as the animal continued to move its head up and down. Then it turned and entered the cattails.

Pretty Weasel jumped up and ran back into the trees. Loney caught up with him and said, "Was it a bear?"

"Oh, yes," he breathed. And he took off running down the treeline, just out of sight of the field.

Loney ran after him. He wanted to ask why that was a bear. There were no bears anymore. They had been driven out of the valley years ago by settlers and hunters. But Pretty Weasel was far ahead.

By the time Loney reached the point in the treeline opposite the stand of cattails, Pretty Weasel was in a shallow draw between the two. He was crouched low to the ground, moving slowly, his rifle close to his chest. Loney decided to wait. He wasn't anxious to go into the cattails, so he squatted with his back against a box elder that grew apart from the cottonwoods and peered through the slim willows that flanked the draw. He put his hands in his pockets and determined not to think about Yellow Eyes.

Instead, he thought that his sister loved him and that he was cold. In the back of his mind, the part he seldom touched, he knew that they would get along better when the weather warmed. People always got along better when the days were hot and the nights cool. The nights took the meanness out of people. He thought of the nights he and Kate had sat on the back porch watching stars appear, one by one, until the mosquitoes drove them indoors. Kate had always found the first star and Loney never caught on until she left that she knew the position of the evening star. She didn't like his friends. Sometimes she didn't like him. But at night, those long summer nights, she loved him and he loved her.

And he thought of Yellow Eyes. Struck by a train, killed beyond recognition, in February of 1963 somewhere in the south of Montana between Bozeman and Butte. Loney had been in Great Falls that winter working for the county and he had read an account of it in the *Tribune,* a small article in one of the back pages which referred to him as the "unidentified man." A couple of days later an even smaller article called him by his real name, George Yellow Eyes. Loney had never mentioned it to anybody and it had apparently not appeared in the *Harlem News.* It was as though Yellow Eyes had disappeared without a trace. Nobody ever said, "Whatever happened to Yellow Eyes?" And Loney had never volunteered his information to anyone, except to Pretty Weasel that morning. Now Loney wondered why he had kept it to himself, but even as he wondered a vague memory touched his mind and he saw this: A late fall evening, two boys walking home from basketball practice, their hair still wet, one of the boys talking earnestly in low rapid tones and the other silent, falling loose at the joints, as he listened to the first boy. And the second boy, when he reached the boardinghouse, was dreadfully tired and went straight to his room and to bed. And he didn't go to school the next day; instead he lay in bed (pretending to be sick) and thought about what the first boy had said. He lay there a long time until it was almost dark and the preacher's wife brought him a bowl of soup and some crackers; then he said to her, "I'm not an orphan," and he allowed himself to admit that the first boy was right. They had a mother in common, Loney's natural mother and Yellow Eyes' stepmother.

Even Kate didn't know that their mother had left their father for Yellow Eyes' father. And Loney never told her. And he had never sought out his mother, nor she her natural son. It had been enough for Loney in those days to know that she existed. He and Yellow Eyes never talked of it again and she eventually left Yellow Eyes' father and she became a dream that one wishes to forget. Loney realized that now; more importantly, he realized that it had not been a dream at all, yet it was the stuff of which dreams are made. A real dream made of shit. Loney thought this. And George Yellow Eyes was dead.

A sudden *pop!* then another *pop!* lifted him from his heels. He tried to see through the willows but they were too dense. Then he was running down the draw, levering a shell into the chamber of the 30–30.

When he reached the cattails he hesitated. They were taller than they looked from the treeline. He thought to call out to Pretty Weasel, but what if he had missed, what if he was still hunting the bear? He stood and listened for the rustle of the cattails or the sound of footsteps. He tried to look through the blond stalks, but they were too thick. So he began to circle to his left, toward the point where they had seen the bear enter. For the first time that day Loney became aware of his own footsteps, the grinding crunch of the grainy flecks of snow as he brought his foot down, then the squeak, like the sound of leather rubbing, as he pushed off. Each step seemed louder than the last in a day that had no other sound, just a brilliant sun and sparkling snow. Now he knew that the bear had been almost blinded by the combination of the two. He tried to keep his eyes focused on the cattails, but even their dull yellow seemed too much in the blinding field.

Loney whistled and it startled him, for it was the whistle they had used when they were kids hunting pheasants and rabbits, a quick *wheet wheet*, then a pause, and in that pause, he forgot the rest of it. There was one other sound they had made to complete the signal, but those days were so long ago and gone. He thought, If I could remember, if I could complete it, Pretty Weasel would either say, "Come ahead," or whistle back that the hunt was still on.

Then he heard the brittle crashing of the dry stalks and he saw the darkness of it, its immense darkness in that dazzling day, and he thrust the gun to his cheek and he felt the recoil and he saw the astonished look on Pretty Weasel's face as he stumbled two steps back and sat down in the crackling cattails.

Loney lowered the 30–30 and whistled to him. *Wheet wheet.* But Pretty Weasel just sat there, one hand around his neck, the other holding his rifle upright. Then Loney saw the blood seeping between Pretty Weasel's fingers. The cattails behind him gave way and he fell back, his rifle falling across his face. He lay fifteen feet away but Loney could smell the blood, faintly metallic, in the crystal air.

23

He didn't know how long he had been sitting, but he found himself looking at the sun in the western sky, his back to the cattails. It had turned cold and the sun barely made the blue snow glisten. Loney knew he had to get up and run away from there. Before him he saw the wide depressions in the crust filled with grains of snow. Unless you had seen it, he thought, you'd never know they were bear prints. That was the trouble with hunting in dry snow—the track was obscured as quickly as it was made. Sometimes you could blow into the track, blow the snow out and see what it was you were tracking; that is, if it had warmed up a little, and the track itself was firm. Once he had seen his father lick his hand and feel in the track, then lift his hand gently and wipe off the sticky snow grains, and the track had been that of a bobcat. They weren't even hunting—they had never hunted together. His father had just shown him for a reason neither understood. His father had never instructed him in anything. In this instance he had simply said, "Bobcat." Loney remembered the day, but he knew neither time nor place nor why. He wiped his eyes on his coat sleeve and thought, But the light was just like this, blue going on gray, the sun just a light on the evening star. And Loney felt cold.

He tried to stand and he felt the pain in his shins and the tops of his feet. He squatted and felt the blood sting its way down through his legs.

He found the 30–30 and picked it up by the barrel and tossed it as far as he could into the cattails. Then he started running north toward what was called the Old Highway, a raised dirt road about a quarter of a mile away. He ran hard, once looking up at the prairies that swelled toward Canada. And he thought of Val Marie. He thought if he continued north he would reach Val Marie. Maybe it would take all night, maybe a week, but it was there and the people there were different. Their lives were good and their farms were the biggest in the world and who cared if they could play basketball? Then he thought, There are no Indians there, or even half-breeds, and he became frightened. He knew he was marked, that it was a matter of time. But for the moment he had all the time in the world and he settled down. Maybe he would make it to Val Marie someday. Those Canucks, they were different. They said "a-boot" instead of "about" and the men combed their hair up away from their ears. Sometimes in the summer they stopped for gas in Harlem. Sometimes they even ate lunch at the Chuck-wagon.

Loney crawled through a fence and he was on the Old Highway. If only they could have played Val Marie, Loney would know what was up there. The only thing he knew was that the streets were clean in Canadian towns. He had heard this from different people and he was glad to think it.

Loney was on the Old Highway running hard toward Harlem, thinking of Val Marie, his body empty and light. He was conscious of nothing those first several miles but his shuddering breath and the impatient beat of his heart: Val Ma-rie, Val Ma-rie, Val Ma-rie, Val Ma-rie.

24

It had been dark for two or three hours by the time Loney raised the lights of Harlem. At first they seemed hazy and run together, but as his eyes adjusted he saw each one a dull blue star against the black horizon that was there. Somewhere behind him the dirt road had changed to pavement. He was still running, his body still light, and the steps came with such ease that he couldn't tell if he was touching the earth. Before him the dark pavement glistened with a stubble of winter frost. He ran past the sign that said WELCOME TO HARLEM, HOME OF THE 1958 CLASS B CHAMPS. He couldn't see it but he knew it in his mind. And he knew that the top left corner of it had warped so that the sign looked like a strange kite about to lift into the sky. But he was afraid to look up, for he was afraid that he would see his imaginary bird among the stars.

3

"I told him this morning."

"How did the old fart take it?"

"He was very good about it. He yelled and screamed and tried to strangle me."

"He's right, you know. I hate to agree with the old bastard, but in this case he's right."

"Of course. I accept total and absolute blame. But I doubt that he will have much trouble replacing me. The woods are full of unemployed teachers."

"You could have told me."

"Colleen, it hasn't been that long! I just made up my mind myself two days ago. I mean, for certain."

Colleen rested her head on the back of the leather and wood sofa. She felt miserable but she determined to be nice. It wasn't easy for her. "I don't blame you," she said. "Living here is like being in exile. Siberia couldn't be a hell of a lot worse. Christ, I feel as if I hadn't a friend in the world." She took a quick sip of her beer. She didn't want to explore the truth in that. "Lucky Lager. Yuck."

"I could get you some wine."

"No, don't bother. Don't waste the good stuff."

"Don't be silly. I love you."

"Do you have any whiskey left over from that party?"

"Would you like some?"

"Get me some, will you, honey? Just a water glass will do, nothing fancy." Colleen closed her eyes. Now she was to be really alone. She hadn't counted on this. Six more months of school. But she would get out of Harlem herself next June. Then she would haul her ass back to the coast, maybe back to Seattle, maybe even to grad school at the University of Washington. But she would probably have to live in her parents' home. The thought depressed her. She had a sister in San Francisco and she got all the ass she wanted. Colleen hated her. But she could go down and live with her for a while.

"Here you are."

Colleen took the drink and studied it. "What is it?"

"Scotch."

"Yowie." She raised the glass. "To all those mean Texas mothers."

Rhea watched her drink. In a way she did love Colleen. In spite of her occasional boozy screw-ups, she had been a loyal friend, perhaps the only friend Rhea had had the past two years. She's been selfish and rude and self-pitying, but I think I do love her. When you get past those defenses she's defenseless. That thin wall of bravado comes tumbling down and she's a little girl. I wonder why she had to build it. And Rhea thought, I know so little about her, after two years. I have learned so little. . . .

"What are you smiling about? Don't you know this is a solemn moment?"

"I had no idea I was smiling." Rhea laughed. "I am going to miss you, Colleen."

"Well, don't. We don't want to set a precedent, now, do we?"

"Now you're the one who's smiling."

"I'm just thinking of all this furniture. Are you sure you want to give it to me?"

"I can't take it with me and I'm certainly not going to leave it for the landlord."

"Couldn't you give it to an orphanage? Isn't there an orphanage around here?"

"Would you like me to?"

"No."

"Okay."

Colleen poked at the ice cube in her drink. "Are you ready for the sixty-four-dollar question?" she said.

"Where am I going, right?"

Colleen sucked on her wet finger and nodded. "That's the first sixty-four-dollar question. They get more lucrative later on."

"Well, first I'm going to go home, stay with my parents for a while, perhaps look up a few friends, take advantage of the cultural climate. . . . I don't know. I might go down to Galveston. I love it down there. I used to go there in the spring and lie in the sun and sweat and eat shrimp. . . ."

"Oh, God—stop it! Don't you know you're driving me crazy?"

"I probably won't do any of those things, except stay with my parents and try to figure things out."

"Do they live in a mansion?"

"Sort of . . ."

"Oh, I envy you. You're so petite, so pretty, so rich, so . . . Southern!"

"Colleen, everybody there is Southern." Rhea laughed. "They're so Southern they would drive you crazy in a week."

"Well, I wouldn't mind strapping on one of those Texas mothers, if you'll pardon my French."

"I hate to say it, but I think you have the wrong impression of Texas men, at least the ones I know."

"I have a hunch you and I would hang out with different crowds down there. Me and Willie and Waylon, singin' the sad ones."

Rhea had been sitting on the carpet. Now she lay back and looked up at the sparkly stucco of the ceiling. She tried to think of something good about going home and she thought of Allen Kauffman, her thesis adviser at SMU and the first man she'd ever had an affair with. There had been a lot of "playing around" and sometimes it ended in bed, but she had never had an affair, with its games, its loveliness, its desperate bad moments, until Allen Kauffman, her intense dark man. She was his empty-headed belle, and they played at this game until it became ordinary and difficult. It ended badly and bitterly, but he had given her her freedom, not from him (although that, too, happened) but from her pretty life. And he had taken her innocence. She had never been empty-headed, but she had a kind of willed innocence that he observed and destroyed. She would not see him when she returned, because they had nothing to give to or take from each other. How awkward it would be, she thought. She felt something like a pioneer woman returning from the wilderness. Yet she was fearful.

"Do you mind if I fix myself another drink? I must confess, I'm getting schnockered. Must have been that beer. Jesus, it's not even four o'clock. But it is—was—the last day of school. Yowie." Colleen stood and patted Rhea on the head. "It's going to be a blue, blue Christmas without you, babe."

"And without you."

"Why don't you let me fix you one?"

"Would you?"

"A bomber. We need it. Which reminds me—you've answered question number two. I think you'll stay in Dallas. You'll become some rich cat's pretty little wife, sending her kids off to school, making sure the hors d'oeuvres are perfectamente and the drapes divine—I can see it all now. And you know something? I don't even envy you. Which is a revelation about myself." Colleen picked up her glass.

"As a matter of fact, I'm thinking about Seattle."

Colleen spit the ice cubes back into her glass. "Seattle!" she said. "Oh, Christ. If you think those Texas men are bad, wait'll you get to Seattle. They're all pale and balding and they drive Volvos. They have full beards and half of them are architects. You'll love it. You'll be up to your ass in salal, and you'll have your own dream home, all cedar and glass, perched on a hill overlooking the Space Needle. You'll end up looking out at the cold fog on Elliott Bay and thinking you should get involved. The American Dream moves west. Rhea Davis rolling bandages. Horse shit."

"Why are you talking like this? A month ago you made Seattle sound so attractive. What's changed? You can't imagine that I would live that kind of life."

Colleen shrugged. "No, I'm sorry. You must forgive me. I'm just upset that you're leaving. It was so sudden." She looked at the ice cubes in her glass. "You'll do all right, kiddo. You have a wonderful grace about you. Just consider these past two years as your bad experience. I sure as hell am."

Rhea watched Colleen walk toward the kitchen. She was walking very steadily and seriously, the way she always did just before she came apart. Poor Colleen.

And poor Rhea. She looked at the three rectangles on the wall above the sofa. She had taken the paintings down, but the rectangles were like apparitions, whiter than the white wall.

Whatever am I going to do with myself?

Rhea looked quickly toward the kitchen and she heard Colleen putting ice in the drinks. She closed her eyes and tried to block out the past two years. She tried not to think of Loney. Then she did say it: "Whatever am I going to do with myself?"

2

Loney stood in the lobby of the New England Hotel and listened to the operator dial the number he had given her.

The old phone booth had given way to a new green phone hung on the wall, and so Loney was naked and nervous. From where he stood he could look into the Chuckwagon Café, which adjoined the lobby, separated by a glass door. He saw the desk clerk sitting at the counter talking to a waitress, a high school girl whose mother owned the café. The desk clerk was wearing a brown shirt, brown slacks and black Wellington boots. He had his legs crossed and Loney could see a skinny bare leg. His name was Alf and he was almost retarded.

Loney heard the phone ringing far off in the wires. He had a handful of quarters and dimes and one nickel. He wished he had got more nickels. Then he heard a click and he said "Hello," and the operator started to say something, but his sister's voice cut them both off.

"This is Katherine Loney. I will be out of town until Friday the twenty-third of December."

And Loney said, "Kate?"

"At the tone please leave a message or your name and number and I will return your call."

"Kate, it's Jim."

"I'm afraid she's not in, sir. Do you wish to leave a message?"

"Wasn't that her?"

"That was a recording. Do you wish to leave a message?"

Loney looked out the large north window and he saw a police car sitting a hundred feet from the intersection of the two streets fronting the hotel.

"Just speak into the telephone, sir. Your voice will be recorded."

Loney studied the police car and he said, "What is today?"

"The twenty-third."

"Shouldn't she be there?"

The operator sighed. "Sir, she said the twenty-third, it is the twenty-third, and that's all I can tell you. She's apparently not there."

Loney carefully placed the receiver on its hook and eased the change into his pocket. His face felt hot and heavy and he leaned against the wall for a moment. It occurred to him that he had shot Pretty Weasel—what was it, two days ago, three?—he had killed a man and had smelled his blood in the winter air. And he knew that he couldn't live as though it hadn't happened. The smell was too strong and the killed man would be with him forever. Eventually, inevitably, he would be caught and sent to the prison down in Deer Lodge, likely for the rest of his life. People had seen him in the bar with Pretty Weasel the night before his death. Maybe that cop across the street didn't know anything now, but it would come out someday, someday when Loney wouldn't expect or want it. It might be in the spring when the snow melted, when McFarland went out to work his fields. It might be sooner—a poacher perhaps, or one of the light airplanes that flew up and down the valley. Somebody would find Pretty Weasel and it would probably happen when Loney least wanted it. They would call it murder. Loney thought how easy it would be to walk over to the car and tell the cop that he had killed a man. It would be almost as simple an act as killing.

Loney saw the bear in the field, its head bobbing as though it beckoned to them. The image spooked him and he thought of the bear not as a bear but as an agent of evil—how else explain the fact that there hadn't been a bear in that valley for years and years?—and on Loney's last purposeful day he had succumbed to that evil.

That it was an accident did not occur to Loney. That the bear, as rare and inexplicable as its appearance had been, was simply a bear did not occur to him either. And so he was inclined to think that what had happened happened because of some quirky and predictable fate. He knew that it could only end badly and he also knew he wanted to postpone it. Because his consciousness had dimmed in the past couple of months, along with his thinking, he didn't know that he had in that moment devised an end of his own. And so he slipped out a side door and hurried down the street toward Kennedy's.

3

The cop sat in the warm car and watched the figure hurrying down the street. Before it turned into Kennedy's Bar it was the only sign of life on the street. Now there was nothing. One of those rare moments on any given day when the two main blocks of town were completely devoid of human sign. The cop had become an expert on the traffic patterns of Harlem. Without looking up he knew that it was between four and four-thirty. He guessed that it was four-twenty. To complete the game he looked at his watch. Four-twenty on the nose.

Shit. He glanced up at the rear-view mirror and bared his teeth. He leaned forward over the steering wheel and grinned. He had noticed that morning the small gray dot on one of his front teeth near the gum. It had depressed him, and as if that wasn't enough, he found out when he reported for duty that he would have to work a double shift, all because of that fucking Myers. All the shifts were screwed up, all because that goddamned Myers came down with hepatitis. He was as yellow as chicken fat and he probably wouldn't be back for another couple of weeks. On any normal day, Painter could go home in forty minutes. He found his off-duty ritual pleasant enough—a shower, a couple of drinks, a TV dinner and TV. Some nights he worked on his model planes and some nights he drank and made long-distance telephone calls to California and old friends. He no longer tried to reach his ex-girlfriend, but he was pretty much over her anyway. She was mostly just a confusing memory four years old. All of the good times were gone and Painter was a cop in Harlem, a pretty good cop who kept the town reasonably secure without alienating too many people. The one person he knew when he came up here, the uncle who got him the job, had gotten himself killed in a traffic accident out north. And so Painter never felt close to, or a part of, the town. The closest he ever came was arresting drunks and sleeping with some of the women. He was proud of neither. He needed a woman, and not just any woman.

He sat back and lit a cigarillo. He had learned the night before that the teacher's last name was Davis. His next-door neighbor, Leo Phipps, taught physical education and coached football at the high school and he had had his eye on Rhea Davis for two years, but she had given him nothing, no encouragement, not even the time of day. But that was okay. She wasn't much in the tits department and he was a tit man. If you were an ass man or a leg man, she would drive you crazy. From the waist down she was stacked.

They had been drinking in the coach's basement, which was paneled and decorated with very small trophies. Leo was drunk and Painter was just tight enough to want to pull on his face. He liked Leo—they hunted and drank together and just lately Painter had turned him on to model airplanes—but in his boozy self-righteous way, he wanted to hurt the coach for talking that way about the woman who enriched his fantasies.

But he restrained himself. He chalked it up to the coach's ignorance. Besides, the coach's wife was one of the first women he had screwed when he came to town. Even though she had long since left Leo, Painter still felt guilty enough to let him run off at the mouth.

He watched a car turn off the main highway on the south end of town. It would be the first of the agency employees. He looked at his watch. Four forty-five. In another couple of hours the town would come alive. Friday night. Tomorrow night was Christmas Eve. And he was going to have to work it. He thought of Rhea Davis's firm legs and he got excited. He rubbed his crotch. "Love," he mouthed to the mirror. In his mind she was still handcuffed to the radiator.

4

Loney stood on the hill listening to the wind that came down from the Arctic Circle. Below, the street lamps were clear and cold. And beneath their blue arc Loney could see the shiny tops of cars and he thought he saw a small knot of people standing in the light from the movie marquee. The figures were like black ants and they moved regularly but slowly, like ants picking over a dead thing. A pair of headlights moved up the street toward the movie house. Two of the ants moved away from the carrion. The car stopped for a moment, then drove on, turning at the corner and speeding off toward the Legion Club. When Loney looked back the marquee lights were out.

He opened the barbed-wire gate to the cemetery and stepped through. He closed it behind him, slipping the wire loop back over the post. It wasn't a very big cemetery—there didn't seem to be more than a hundred graves—and Loney wondered where the rest of the dead were buried. He had passed the cemetery countless times in his years but he had never realized how small it was.

There were only about a dozen headstones. Loney lit a match at each one, shielding the flame with his hand, reading each name. But they were the vaguely familiar names of merchants and prominent citizens. When the wind blew out his match at the last headstone, Loney straightened up and glanced around at the other graves. Most of them had either concrete or wooden crosses. A few were marked only by a small hump in the brown weeds.

Loney squatted with his back to the wind and lit a cigarette. He wasn't disappointed, because he hadn't expected to find it. He felt only a small virtue that he had looked for her grave. Her name was Sandra and she had sheltered him. Loney knew now that he would never find her and he was grateful that he hadn't reached his sister that afternoon. He had wanted to ask her if she knew Sandra's surname and where she was buried, but the questions would have been cruel. Kate was suffering enough because of him.

Loney smoked and allowed himself to explore the intricacies of the relations of the people in his life. His own life was not complicated but his mind became confused when he tried to understand what all these people meant to each other and to himself. His mother left his father for Yellow Eyes' father. That's what Yellow Eyes had told him that day years ago after basketball practice. As stunning as the news was, he had accepted it, finally. But he couldn't accept the idea that she had never tried to see him. She had remained in Harlem for some time—why hadn't she tried to see him? Or Kate? He had heard that his mother had gone crazy and he never felt responsible or guilty about it, but he had felt that maybe he could have prevented it if they had only known each other. If they could have talked and looked at each other, maybe she wouldn't have needed to go crazy. And what about his father? What had he done to prevent it? He had taken a lover and her name was Sandra. And after he left, Sandra had taken Loney in. And Kate had refused to live with Sandra.

Loney dropped his cigarette on a mound before him. It skittered away in the harsh wind, its orange glow disappearing behind the mound. I really did try to love Sandra, he thought, but I don't. I didn't know her and it's impossible to love somebody you don't know. He wondered if his father had loved her; or if he had loved Loney's mother. As he tried to strike another match to light a cigarette, he realized that his hands were trembling. He wanted to believe that they trembled because of the cold, but he knew without thinking it that they trembled because there was no real love in his life; that somehow, at some time, everything had gone dreadfully wrong, and although it had something to do with his family, it had everything to do with himself.

5

Rhea sat in the armchair and watched Colleen sleep. She wanted to feel high but she just felt worthless. She wanted to be gone, to be on the road, in Denver, Amarillo, anywhere but here. She had loaded her car that afternoon before Colleen showed up. Thank God for that, she thought. It made her a little giddy to think that all she had to do in the morning was get in the car, start the motor and drive away. But with her pictures gone, her clothes and books and stereo set packed and her small things in an overnight bag, she felt lost and strange, as though she were a stranger in this town she had spent two years trying to live with.

She walked into the kitchen to fix herself another drink. She wanted to get drunk. She wanted to pass out like Colleen. She wanted mostly to be gone. I want so many things, she said to the refrigerator. I didn't find them here. I won't find them in Dallas. As she put the ice in her glass, she thought how wonderful it would be to be in a motel room in Billings or Cheyenne, somewhere on the map, in transit.

She tiptoed back into the living room. She had changed into her nightgown. Fortunately she had had the presence of mind to leave out her best gown, a peach-colored silk, and as she felt the thick carpet beneath her bare feet, she thought of herself as a nymph, so delicate and light that the moss scarcely stirred. And she thought, Oh, I'm thinking in a Dallas way already.

Colleen had rolled over onto her back on the rug, her gangly legs spread beneath the hiked-up skirt. Rhea put her drink on the coffee table and carefully removed Colleen's glasses. Before she turned away she looked down at Colleen's legs. There was a run in her panty hose that started at the left knee and continued up her thigh. Oh, lord. Rhea stepped back and giggled. We are sad women. And she laughed aloud and she put her hands to her face and continued laughing. I shouldn't laugh, she thought, and she thought of something else and she did stop. She dabbed at her eyes with a Kleenex and listened a moment and heard Colleen say, "What's up, hon?"

"Nothing. Go back to sleep." But she knew that Colleen had not wakened.

Then she heard the wind rattle the glass doors. She had become used to the north wind in her two years, but tonight it meant something. After tonight she would never know that particular wind again.

6

Ike Loney poured the oil into the reservoir behind the small stove. He hated the smell of heating oil. He wished he had an electric blanket to wrap around himself. Then he wouldn't have to heat the whole goddamn trailer. But there wasn't much to the trailer—a table and two benches in front, a galley in the middle and a bed in the rear. Beside the bed, a cubicle contained a toilet and a shower nozzle.

The radio on the table was tuned to Havre. He hated the Havre station, but until late night, it was all he could get. He wanted to hear voices talking, but all he heard from Havre were voices singing and advertising. Later he would be able to get a Salt Lake station and an all-night talk show. Then he would get into bed and listen and scoff at the amateur experts. Everybody had an opinion and it made him laugh. But he never missed the program and the voices made him feel normal.

Ike sat down and cut himself a slice of American cheese. He wished he had himself a television. To actually see people would be a hell of a lot better than just listening to them. He would love to see that talk show host. Sometimes he envisioned him as fat and kind of bald; at other times as wiry, with wiry black hair. Kind of a testy little runt. Jesus, what kind of home life does he have? Probably one of them goddamn Mormons. Naw, they wouldn't be talking about abortions as if it was the same thing as going down to the drugstore for an ice cream cone. I'll bet he's a Jew, Ike thought. Be just like them. Rattle on for hours about cutting a baby out of its poor mother's womb. Then go home in the morning for some bacon and eggs. Ike had grown to recognize some of the callers, like the cookie woman, who was always calling up to ask if the host had got those cookies she sent him. Or that so-called expert on clouds.

Ike chewed his cheese for a long time. He wasn't as broke as some of the folks around there thought, and that knowledge contented him. He was getting $162 a month disability for screwing up his back. The pain hardly bothered him anymore and it had allowed him to come back to Harlem and live all right. Once or twice, in the beginning, he had felt a little guilty about sponging drinks off of Kenny, but the feeling passed. What the hell, he thought, a few beers. What's that worth to a friendship as long as ours? Maybe it wasn't a real friendship anymore; maybe it never had been; but Ike and Clancy Peters used to let Kenny tag along when they went out to raise hell. That was worth something.

Poor old Clancy. He ain't nothing anymore. All busted up from rodeoing, sugar diabetes. Be hard to tell some of these kids around here that in his day he was tops. Now he gets his ass chewed off by that loudmouth woman he's living with.

Ike glanced at the clock on top of the refrigerator. Nine thirty-five. At ten o'clock he would go downtown to help Kenny close the place up. He continued to chew the American cheese.

7

Loney stood at the end of the street and stared at the trailer. At night it looked even more remote, as though it had never been intended to be a part of the town. And its teardrop shape suggested that it should be moving, that it was not meant to be still. But there was a life to it, lights in the window and smoke blowing directly south from the chimney. Loney struck a match, cupping both hands around it, and stuck his cigarette into the opening between his thumbs. Then he opened his hands and the flame disappeared. He wanted to stay there and smoke the cigarette, but he was desperately cold. He touched his face and it felt like rubber. He couldn't tell if the feeling was gone from his hands or his face or both. He flicked the cigarette into the wind and walked across the small field to the trailer. When he knocked he couldn't feel that either.

And when the door opened Loney recognized the white shirt and baggy suit pants. The face was in the shadows above him, away from the lamp over the kitchen table. Loney smelled the oil stove and he heard the music. Then he heard his father's voice: "What the hell's going on out here?"

And Loney said, "I'm cold."

The old man left the door open and walked back to the table. He sat down facing Loney. As cold as he was, Loney thought of closing the door and walking away. He smelled the oil and it made him feel sick. But because he was cold and because the door was open, he stepped up into the trailer.

"Close the door," his father said. "Close it tight."

Loney pulled the door until he heard it latch behind him. He glanced around the inside of the trailer and he felt gigantic. His father said, "You want some cheese?" And Loney said, "Yes." Then he squeezed into the booth opposite the old man.

Ike cut a thick slice off the loaf of pasteurized cheese, stuck it with the knife blade, then shook it off on the table before Loney. Loney tried to pick it up but his fingers felt big and clumsy. It's the cold. He felt foolish. He put his hands under the table and flexed them, trying to regain the feeling. His face became hot. He wanted to tell the old man how cold it was outside, but he couldn't presume too much. He watched his father fiddle with the station selector on the radio and he heard the bits and snatches of music as it made its way across the lighted dial. "All I get's this goddamn music. It's no good." Then Ike picked up a station that was delivering the news. "You know how many times I've heard the news today? Twelve times. Why did you come here?"

"To talk."

"About what?"

Loney thought a moment. "About the last thirty-five years."

Ike stopped fooling with the radio. He looked at the man across the table and his eyes narrowed. "How old are you?"

"Thirty-five."

Ike picked the knife up from the table. He leaned back and ran his thumb over its edge. "How old am I?"

"Around sixty, I think."

"Sixty-two. Now why did you come here?"

"I want you to tell me some things."

"What do I know that you'd want? I'm an old man. I was born to buck and broke to ride. It's all over."

"I want you to tell me about my mother—who she was, what she was like and where she is. You can tell me that for now."

Ike set the knife on the table. "Damn," he said. "Damn you." For he had thought of his wife again, the second time in the past few days. Something's at work here, he thought. Here I go half my life without a thought of her and now I'm not only thinking about her, but so's this kid. Maybe there was something to it. "She was a whore," he said.

"What do you mean?"

"Just that. She was a whore." Ike stood up and walked a couple of steps to the stove. He removed the cap and looked down into the reservoir. "Goddamn it. I fill this thing up half an hour ago and it's down by half already." He walked another two steps into the kitchen and opened one of four tiny cupboards hanging from the roof of the trailer.

Loney watched him take a bottle from the cupboard. It was a pint of whiskey. It had no label and the whiskey was the color of rust. The fact that his father had an undrunk pint around surprised him. The fact that the old man had two glasses in his other hand surprised him even more.

"Now we'll see how tough you are. I got this off a Polack down in Butte, only Polack left in Butte. Now they're all Micks and Finns. He called this stuff Polish vodka. Truth is, I've been a little afraid to drink it. Truth is, I'm afraid it's poisont."

"What if it is?" said Loney as he watched his father pour.

"Well then, I guess you and me will perish together."

Ike made a gesture as if to toast his son; then he threw the whiskey down. It was strong but smooth. He had his son's number. Ike felt it all the way down and it was good. "You know I'm not supposed to drink this stuff? Yeah, supposed to kill me. I don't give a shit, though."

"Did she run around? Is that what you mean?"

"What the hell are you asking these questions for? Christ, he hasn't seen me for twenty years and he has to know everything all of a sudden. We'll get there, don't worry. What the hell's the hurry, anyway?"

"I've seen you lots in the last fourteen years. You've seen me too."

"Was that you?" Ike laughed and he felt good and reckless. He had felt it coming on and the drink of whiskey set him up.

Loney looked at his father. He was older now, and scrawnier, but he was the same man who had walked out the door twenty-five years before. It was only at this moment that Loney remembered he and Kate had been terrified of him. He had been a bully then and it seemed he had not changed. And Loney felt an old hatred stirring within him, as though the twenty-five years had been nothing more than a bird disappearing in the night. Loney was not terrified anymore.

"She left you because you were no good."

"Who's to say she didn't leave because of you? She left just after you were born. Hell, she hardly even suckled you and that was too long. Besides, who's to say I didn't kick her out? I should have kicked the whole works of you out, but I was different then. I had a soft heart in those days."

Loney declined to be drawn into a fight. He hadn't come to fight. "Where did she go then?"

"She stuck around town, kept begging me to take her back."

"She went to live with George Yellow Eyes' father."

"As a last resort. When she saw I wasn't going to give in, she went over and shacked up with him. She was like that."

Loney took a sip of his whiskey. He listened to the north wind whistle over the stovepipe above them. He didn't believe his father. She wouldn't have begged him. "What did she look like?"

"Oh ho ho—when I first laid eyes on her she was the prettiest damn girl you ever saw. Jesus, she was fresh in from Lodgepole and she didn't know shit from Shinola. She was working over at the agency in the hospital—I don't know, some kind of nurse's helper. She was maybe seventeen, eighteen at the time. I used to drive over there, me and Clancy Peters—he had one of the first automobiles in this county—and we were both sort of courting her. Well, to make a long story short, I won out. . . ." Ike watched his hand guide the knife blade through the loaf of cheese. He cut the loaf in half. "She was as pretty as you please, full-blooded Gros Ventre, didn't hardly say a word in those days. She was kind of like a sleek animal. First time I saw her was at a powwow over on the other side of the agency. Jesus, it was hot and dusty, me and Clancy were about half drunk on that bootleg stuff old Forgie used to sell, and I just couldn't take my eyes off of her. She was like an animal, all dressed up in doeskin—dress, leggings, the whole works. She danced real slow, the way the women used to in those days, just one foot in front of the other, never turning her head left or right, never letting on there were others in the circle. Between dances she would sit alone under a lodgepole shelter. The other girls would be giggling and flirting with some of the young bucks, but not Eletra. She didn't engage in that kind of stuff, not in those days. Clancy and me, we decided to go over there and get a better look at her, but those goddamn bucks run us out of there. We thought about engaging them, but it was a religious ceremony and everything—you seldom saw a white man on that reservation in those days. Anyway, I found out a couple of days later that she worked in the hospital and I started going around there. She stole my heart. And I won out too."

Loney smoked a cigarette and watched the old man slice

the loaf of cheese into pieces, then slice the pieces into ribbons. He sipped at his drink and wondered if it was all a fantasy—him sitting with his father, his father telling a story about a woman he had never met but who bore him. He wondered if his father hadn't made up this woman. She wasn't the crazy woman Loney had heard about.

But his father said, "I don't know what happened after those first couple of years. She just sort of went to hell. Started drinking, running around, lost her looks. . . ."

"It was because you made her that way. You ruined her—if she was as good in the beginning as you say."

"Like hell."

"You couldn't help yourself. You can't help the way you are."

"Bullshit."

"Don't take it personally."

"Don't take it personally, he says. Calls me a horse's ass and says, Don't take it personally."

"Don't be mad. I want you to tell me other things. Here, we'll have another drink."

"Offers me a drink of my own booze."

"Here, we'll toast: To the way we are."

"Now what's the matter?"

"Nothing."

"You've got tears in your eyes. Jesus, you're crying, just like a baby."

"No, I'm not crying. Now you must tell me more. Tell me—what was my mother's name before you married her?"

"I thought that sister of yours would have told you. She seems to have the line on everything."

"She didn't. Yes, yes, she said our mother was a Westwolf."

"Westwolf, hell. There aren't even any Westwolfs out in that part of the country."

"Then what was her name?"

"Eletra. Eletra Calf Looking."

"Eletra," said Loney.

"She was as good a goddamn woman as the good lord ever put on this poor earth," said Ike.

Loney laughed.

"What's so funny about that?"

"Nothing." Loney laughed.

"You have a mighty peculiar way of respecting other people's feelings."

"I'm not laughing about that. I'm sorry. I'm just laughing—it's the way I am these days. And now—where is she now? No, I'm not laughing. Where is she right this minute?"

"First he's bawling like a baby and now he's laughing like a hyena," Ike said to the radio. "Now he wants to know where his mother is after all these years."

"I want you to tell me."

"If you think I know, then why don't you? You always were kind of a smartass kid."

"I'm not that way anymore."

"Last I heard she was down in New Mexico. She's a nurse or something in one of them reservation hospitals."

"A nurse!"

"What's so unusual about that? She was practically a nurse when I first met her."

Loney looked at his father. He wanted to know if his father was joking, but his expression hadn't changed. He continued to slice the cheese into small squares. He actually looked miserable.

"I'd have thought she'd be on the skids," said Loney. "Like us. Like you and me."

"I'd watch whose reputation I was tarnishing if I was you. One of us isn't quite as bad off as the other thinks. That's my advice to you." And Ike allowed himself a small grin.

"Is she happy?" said Loney. "Is she happy down there in New Mexico?"

"That I couldn't tell you. I don't make it my business to go around opening old cans of worms."

"She must be happy. I'll bet she's very happy. And why shouldn't she be—she's rid of us. I'll bet she's got a boyfriend down there. I'll bet he's a doctor. I'll bet she helps him give shots and examine teeth. What a secret!" Loney laughed.

"You're crazy," said his father.

"And what about Sandra? Is she a nurse too?"

Ike swallowed his drink. He looked at the radio, but he didn't talk to it. "You really know how to stick it to your father, don't you?" he said.

"Here, let me pour you another. After all, this is a reunion, a celebration of sorts. Okay, we're all set, you and me. Now we'll talk some more. If she wasn't a nurse, what was she to you and me? Kate said she was your lover. But how? How did she love you? Maybe she was an angel. Tell me, was she an angel?"

A gust of wind made the damper on the oil stove hum. From somewhere far off a dog barked, and its bark was carried away. And Ike realized that every night of his life he had heard a dog bark. Some summer nights the dogs barked until dawn. I shouldn't have lied to him, he thought. I shouldn't have told him that his mother was a nurse in New Mexico. Damn, now he's got the drop on me. He knows I lied. That's why he's acting so goddamn smart. He knows his mother is crazy. He thinks I put her in that damn bughouse.

"If she wasn't an angel, what was she?"

"Who?"

"Sandra. Who else were we talking about?"

"She came along at the right time. I guess you could call her something of an angel."

"How so?"

Ike laughed, but there was no joy in it. "She was a social worker. She was a white woman but she worked for the agency. She came over to the house one day, had this idea I wasn't taking care of you kids. Well, before she left I had poured the coals to her. She wasn't thinking about you kids then, I'll tell you. Oh, I don't mean I changed her whole way of thinking; I just gave her a new set of priorities."

Loney suddenly felt sick from the cheese, the smell of oil and the whiskey. The light from the lamp above the table had begun to hurt his eyes and he felt overwhelmed by the closeness of the trailer. He didn't want to go on with this talk—he wanted to get out into the cold air—but it was necessary that they finish. "Then you ran out on her," he said, and his voice sounded weary to him.

"I wasn't ready to get trapped again. I'd already been trapped by one woman, saddled with a couple of kids. . . . You can understand that." Ike looked into Loney's face for the understanding he deserved, and he found nothing. "I'd already been through a bum marriage—Jesus, I was just about your age. I had nothing left to give a woman. So I decided to get away. That's when I left for Butte." Again he looked into Loney's face. "Try to put yourself in my shoes. I was just about your age."

But Loney couldn't put himself in his father's shoes. He was confused and he felt like a child again, and he remembered as a child he had run his fingers through Sandra's hair and had felt like a man. But he hadn't been a man. His father had been a man and had "poured the coals to her." That ability was what made a man. Loney felt a kind of distant shame for having thought up until now that he had been a kind of lover to Sandra. He had deluded himself all these years.

"Why did she take me in after you left?"

Loney's father laughed again. "She was a social worker, wasn't she? Didn't I just tell you that?"

Loney picked up a small cube of cheese. He studied its perfection. It had dried to the consistency of putty. He squashed it and four small fissures appeared where the corners had been. "Was that the only reason?" he said.

"Far as I know. Like I told you, I left for a new life."

"Then you don't know what happened to her?"

"Nope."

"Kate said she's dead. Maybe a car accident. You don't know?"

But his father was fiddling with the dials on the radio.

Loney poured himself another drink of the rusty booze. He wiped the sweat from his forehead and thought briefly of taking his parka off, but the act seemed too much like a commitment. He had come as a stranger to a stranger for information, he hadn't come as a son. So he sipped his whiskey and watched Ike tune in a reluctant station. It was a talk show, a long way off.

"Here's this sonofabitch now," Ike muttered.

But Loney wasn't listening. His thoughts had turned a corner and he no longer thought or cared about his mother or the social worker. He had felt when he entered the trailer that there had to be an explanation to their existences, and his father had given him nothing. In a way, Loney thought, this old man is innocent. He knows nothing, he cares nothing, and that makes him innocent.

And Loney knew who the guilty party was. It was he who was guilty, and in a way that made his father's past sins seem childish, as though original sin were something akin to stealing candy bars.

8

"I killed a man," said Loney. His mother and the social worker were gone now, wiped clean from his mind.

Ike looked up from the radio.

"I killed Pretty Weasel," said Loney. "I shot him with a thirty-thirty. I thought he was a bear."

Ike frowned, as though he didn't know whether those words were coming from the radio or his son.

"Pretty Weasel," his son said. "Myron."

"You what?"

"With a thirty-thirty. I thought he was a bear. The sun blinded me."

Ike turned down the radio. He was irritated. He didn't believe his son, but he said, "Do the cops know?"

"Not yet. I suppose that's next."

"Shouldn't you tell them?"

"I suppose."

"Are you on the run?"

"I suppose."

"Was it an accident? It must have been an accident."

"I don't know. I think it was, but I don't know for sure."

"You mean you might have done it on purpose?"

"Yes."

Ike looked at the radio, then at his son. His eyes narrowed. "Are you on the level—about the whole business?"

"As God is my witness."

"You and God don't travel in the same circles." But Ike was definitely thrilled. "Holy Jesus."

"Should I tell them?"

"Wait a minute. Let me think. It was an accident, you say?"

"Maybe."

"Great. For the sake of argument, let's say it *was* an accident. What's the worst they can do to you?"

"Throw me in jail."

"They could hang you. I heard on the radio they're going to start hanging men again. Fuck the Supreme Court. Who can blame them?"

Loney squashed another piece of cheese between his fingers.

He wondered if he had really meant to tell his father this thing. He wondered if that was really why he had come here.

"Self-defense. He was coming at you with a gun—did he have a gun? You had no choice. . . ."

"I think I killed him on purpose," said Loney.

"Then you must run. That's it. You must run away from here, lose yourself in a city—Seattle, Portland, California!" Ike was excited by the prospect. He had only gotten as far as Butte. But he hadn't killed a man. He watched his son light a cigarette. Jesus, he's a pretty cool customer. Shoots a man and acts like nothing's wrong. He stood and emptied the ashtray into a paper sack beside the stove. "Sit there," he said, and walked back into his bedroom.

Loney watched him drop stiffly to all fours and rummage around under the bed. He watched his father sit back on his haunches and do something close to his chest. Then the old man slid halfway under the bed again.

He returned to the kitchen and dropped three new twenty-dollar bills on the table before Loney. All three curled cylindrically, as though they had been wrapped around something for some time. "You take this," Ike said. "Get on the bus and don't stop until it runs out. It'll get you to the coast."

Loney looked at the money. His father's generosity bewildered him, first with the whiskey, now with the money. He wondered if this was a virtue his father had always possessed.

"I don't think I'm going to need it."

"What? You're so goddamn rich?" Ike was surprised and hurt. "It's good, it's real." He snatched up the bills and put a lengthwise crease in them. "How's that?"

And Loney said, "I'm not going away." Then he added, as the thought struck him, "I'm going to the Little Rockies." Then he added again, "Up Mission Canyon. I'm going to think."

"Why there? It's winter, for Christ's sake."

But Loney couldn't answer. He had been to Mission Canyon twice in his life: once with the minister and his wife on a picnic, and once with Rhea. But he thought, That's where I'll go, that's the best place. "Mission Canyon," he said again to make sure that his father knew. It was part of a dim plan that he didn't understand. "Mission Canyon," he said, and he watched his father fold the bills and put them in his shirt pocket. The shirt was so thin that the pocket turned the green of the money.

Ike stood without a word and walked back again to the bedroom. He opened a tall narrow closet and took out a long object wrapped in an army blanket. Then he reached higher in the closet and he had a box in his hand. Loney saw the shells first, and when his father sat down, the army blanket fell away and the object was his father's sixteen-gauge. "You might need this," said his father. "There might be some grouse up there." And Loney watched a familiar grin stretch itself across the old man's face.

He took the gun. It was a Remington pump and it looked and felt just as it had in his dream, the cold blue barrel, the smooth grip of the forearm and stock. For a moment everything went away and Loney said, "It's a perfect bird gun," and he felt foolish and triumphant in saying it.

And his father said, "You might see some grouse," and he grinned. He felt a part of something bigger than his life.

Loney took four shells out of the box and pushed them up into the magazine. Then he closed the flap of the box and sat with the gun against his left thigh. Under the glaring lamp he saw that much of the bluing had worn off the barrel. It was an old gun, probably twenty-five or thirty years old.

Ike poured the remaining whiskey into their glasses, then threw the empty bottle into the garbage sack. "I guess it ain't poisont," he said.

They sat and drank slowly, silently. Once Loney said, "Don't you think we could have done something together—if you had stuck around, if we had stuck together?" And Ike said, "Shit, what would we have done but drink ourselves to death?"

9

Loney walked across the yard to where the road began. His head was very clear and the night was clear and cold. The wind had died to an icy breeze on his cheek. The shotgun lay in the crook of his arm and he nibbled a piece of tired cheese. As he walked, he found himself longing for summer and the evening breeze that brought with it the odors of dusty growing things. Winters were too harsh and unremitting, and caused people to behave badly.

When he reached the road he pumped a shell into the chamber and turned. He put the gun to his cheek and sighted at the small yellow window. He felt the recoil and his eyes snapped shut. When he opened them, the window was dark and he could see the tattered curtains blowing aimlessly. He pumped another round into the chamber and when the porch light in a house fifty feet away came on, he threw the gun to his shoulder and blew it out. For just an instant he smelled the gunpowder before the wind carried it away. He had heard neither explosion and he knew that the wind had blown the noise toward town. He turned in that direction and hurried down off the road and up over the railroad tracks. He stopped in the lee of a grain elevator and lit a cigarette.

10

She had just gotten into bed. Her thoughts had tired her and she felt she could sleep now. Nothing resolved, she thought, but sleep. And sleep will work. It is magic to close one's eyes and die for just a little while. A crazy thought. And tomorrow I will be gone.

That's when she heard the doorbell, the quick *bing bong.* It was a civilized noise of intrusion, unlike wind or the rattle of trains. Again, *bing bong.* She had packed her robe, a dumb thing, so she hurried down the hall to the closet by the door. She quietly removed her coat from a hanger and put it on over her nightgown. "Who is it?" she called, and she half expected to hear the voice of the school principal, miserable old Gaetano, who had been enraged by her leaving that morning.

But there was no answer. She opened the door as far as the chain lock would allow and she saw Loney's thin face in the moonlit night. His nose and cheekbones were silver and his eyes were dark caves. She took the chain off the door and opened it.

Loney looked back toward the street.

"Come in," she whispered. But she didn't want him to. Lord, she didn't want him to. "Come into the bedroom." And she saw the shotgun, which he held pointed down against his leg.

She closed the door behind them, glanced into the living room, where Colleen still lay sleeping, then led him down the hallway. In the bedroom she said, "Why do you have that gun?"

And he said, "It's my father's."

And she said, "Why?"

"I'm going hunting," he said. Then he said, "I came to say goodbye."

Rhea looked into the dresser mirror and ran her hand through her hair. Her eyes looked small to her without mascara. For an instant she thought of putting some on.

But Loney had been glancing around the room. It was bare, except for a beauty bag on the dresser and a shirt and pants hanging in the open closet. "You're leaving too," he said.

"Forever. For all time. But you're not going hunting." Rhea suddenly felt her shoulders twitch violently, as though she had just understood the implications of the gun, which she had, and she expected the worst. She couldn't take her eyes off the barrel, which glistened sharply in the yellow light. "Why the gun?" And her voice trembled.

But Loney turned and leaned the gun against the wall by the door. "It belonged to my father. He gave it to me. He wanted me to have it."

"You talked to your father?"

"Yes."

"You went to see him?"

"We had a good time. We split a bottle of whiskey and talked and laughed. We had a fine time."

Rhea sank to the edge of the bed and sighed with relief. She couldn't have believed that he would use the gun. She couldn't have believed that of him.

"Everything's okay now," said Loney.

"Oh, good," said Rhea. "Oh, good for you." She reached for his hand and pulled him down beside her. "I'm so pleased."

Loney looked at her and she *was* pleased. He was glad he had lied. Her eyes were bright with pleasure and she touched him on the cheek. She looked cool and perfect to him. If I could have been someone else, Loney thought, if I had some sort of peace, perhaps we could have done it. This room, so clean and warm, we could have slept here every night, and in the morning, in the morning we would wake up and see each other. . . . He clutched her hand and he knew it was too late, they would both be gone in the morning, and his heart sank as he thought the morning, too, would be gone forever.

Rhea pulled her hand free and put her arm around him and pulled his head down to her small breasts. She felt his cheek, still cold, against the peach-colored gown. She held him and she was glad he had lied to her about his father. In spite of the gun, it had made her feel for a moment that something good could happen in this town.

11

"Have you eaten anything today?" She sat cross-legged on the bed. She was naked, and content for the first time in two weeks to be where she was. She would leave in the morning, nothing had changed, but now there was none of that dreadful anticipation. She felt warm and free of it.

Loney, too, was naked and moonlight touched his body with silver. He was standing, looking out the small high window toward the Little Rockies. He had been thinking he should leave, but he wanted to be with Rhea for a while longer.

"I have a confession to make," she said.

Loney lay back down on the bed and touched her knee.

"Colleen is passed out in the living room. She came by this afternoon and started drinking. Now I'm afraid she's dead to the world—and to us." Rhea giggled.

Loney smiled in the dark. He touched her ribs and she fell on top of him, giggling into his neck, and he loved her breasts on his chest. "You should choose your friends more carefully," he said.

"Don't I just know it. And you, Mr. Loney, are a case in point."

"I do know," he said.

She bit his neck.

"I would have given more to you if I could," he said.

"Oh, Jim, you've been wonderful," she said, her voice soft and Southern. "We've been wonderful."

Loney stared up at the ceiling. He felt he was in a dream and he was conscious only of Rhea's weight on his chest. He heard nothing and he saw nothing and he liked it like that.

"I do love you," she said, her voice drifting.

And he almost said it too, but there was no place to take it.

"I must make you something to eat. You must be so hungry." Her voice came from a long way off. He held her tight and he knew that she had loved him. He kissed her hair and closed his eyes. I have to leave, he thought, but he held her as though to prevent her from slipping away.

12

He woke up and it was still dark and he was very hungry, but the idea of food made him sick. Except for a piece of cheese, he hadn't eaten in the two or three days since killing Pretty Weasel. He lay on his back and felt a pale sweat tingle on his forehead and his upper lip. He would have to try to eat something.

He slipped into his pants and shirt and then, remembering Colleen in the living room, he pulled his socks on. He didn't feel much toward her, but she made him uncomfortable. He couldn't believe that they had once made love in her car down at the Dodson fair. But it hadn't really been an act of love, just a quick coming together, and he had left her sprawled in the back seat while he went to drink beer with his cronies under the rodeo stands. That had been three years ago. He had been a different man then. He never really had friends, but he had cronies, and a couple of women he saw every once in a while, whenever he needed to. And whenever he needed money, he worked, putting up hay for ranchers, fighting fire with an Indian crew, laboring for the railroad, the highway. It wasn't much of a life, but he had done those things, and when he bathed he had felt clean, and when he walked downtown he had looked forward to something. Maybe that was it. The "something" never happened and he had ceased to look for it. But why couldn't he have gone on with that life? The others, his cronies, did, and given the wear and tear of years, had survived. Somewhere along the line he had started questioning his life and he had lost forever the secret of survival.

The light above the sink was on. He steadied himself against the counter and looked down into the white basin. He was very weak and he didn't want to be. He held his hands against the sink and his arms twitched. His knees collapsed forward against the cupboard door beneath the fixture. He stood that way until his arms stopped twitching, and then he found a glass and he drank water. He drank three glasses of water and he felt his stomach tighten and he thought he could eat something. He found a half loaf of bread in the refrigerator. He took a slice and brought it to the light and he remembered the sandwiches he and Kate had made as kids—mustard sandwiches, mayonnaise sandwiches, butter sandwiches, pepper sandwiches—but he remembered most the doughballs. Now he crushed the bread in his fist, kneading it, until it was small and round and moist. He and Kate used to pretend that the doughballs were cookies. Once they ate a whole loaf of doughballs.

He put the doughball in his mouth and chewed, but it tasted like nothing. He needed it to be a game, to pretend that it was something, but it tasted flat and gummy. He washed it down with water. Then he got another slice of bread. The only other thing in the refrigerator was a bowl of eggs. They were large and brown. One of them had a small feather stuck to its shell. Loney pulled the feather free and thought, She gets her eggs from the Hutterites. Many people in town did because the eggs were better and cheaper than store-bought eggs. It didn't surprise him that Rhea bought her eggs from the Hutterites, but it did interest him and faintly hurt him that he hadn't known. There were so many simple things about her that he didn't know, and yet he knew her eyes, her voice, her body. He knew her but he didn't know much about her. He glanced around the kitchen and he saw two hotpads hanging beside the stove and he realized that he hadn't seen them before. Of course they had always been there. In many ways, he hadn't.

And he saw the bottle of Scotch. It was a half gallon with three or four inches left. He poured out his water and poured some of the Scotch into the glass. It tasted harsh and good and he felt it descend and warm him as his wine never had. He had left doughballs and make-believe far behind.

Back in the bedroom he pulled his shoes on and tied them. Then he shrugged into his parka. Suddenly Rhea said, "Tomorrow the world!" She said it clearly and dramatically, the way she did when she was being pompous for him. He looked toward the bed, but she hadn't moved. Her shoulder and back were satiny in the moonlight. She had been dreaming. Loney smiled as he pulled the covers over her body. He didn't touch her. He couldn't let himself touch her again.

He stood in the doorway with the shotgun in the crook of his arm, and in an odd way he felt that he was sparing her life. And more than that, he felt that he was giving her her life. "Goodbye," he whispered, and he didn't weep and he didn't feel corny.

He hurried down the hallway to the kitchen, where he screwed the cap on the Scotch bottle. Then he tucked it up under his parka and left, out of the warmth and into a cold moony night.

13

"You want to tell these fellows exactly what you told me, Mr. Loney?"

"Who are they?"

"Well, we have Chief Hanson of the Harlem police department, a couple of fellows from the Montana highway patrol, and Mr. Doore of the reservation police."

Ike Loney had a large bandage over his eyes. Beneath the bandage his eyes were open. He couldn't shut them because of the glass splinters. The public health doctor had removed most of the glass from his face, but he was reluctant to work on Ike's eyes, so they were waiting for someone to wake up the ambulance driver to take him to Havre.

"You just tell it like it is, Mr. Loney," said Painter. He had finally calmed down. He had taken the call from the old man's neighbor that a madman had been shooting up the street with a shotgun. When he got to the scene he found Ike wandering around outside his trailer. His face was a mask of blood, and Painter had thought that the madman had blown it away. He had actually jumped back into his car when the old man approached. He had lost his cool completely. He just wasn't cut out for the real bad stuff.

"We're police officers," said Chief Hanson.

"We're here to enforce the law," said one of the highway patrolmen.

"One of you fellows got some chewing gum?" said Ike.

Painter studied the old man's face. It wasn't so bad now, except for the white welts where the doctor had removed the shards. He recognized the face. He had seen it several times down at Kennedy's when he made his bar rounds.

"How about a cigarette?" said Mr. Doore.

"Aw, shit," said Ike.

"Okay, let me see if I've got this straight, Mr. Loney—"

"Not so loud, Painter. It's his eyes, not his ears," said Chief Hanson.

"Your boy came to visit you, you gave him a couple of drinks, he got rowdy, stole your shotgun and shot the shit out of your trailer." Painter waited. He knew that Hanson wouldn't like that little profanity, but it was the old man's word. Vivid as hell, thought Painter. He had grown to admire old Loney. He hadn't complained once, hadn't even said ouch.

Ike had told Painter the whole story during the ride over to the agency hospital, or almost the whole story. He had left out the best part. He was waiting to spring it on them at the right time.

"And then he took off. Where was it, Mr. Loney, that you said he was heading?"

"I don't know. He said something about the mountains." Ike felt crafty.

"Did he say which mountains—the Little Rockies, the Bearpaws?"

"Yeah, I think he mentioned something about the Little Rockies." Ike straightened and shifted his buttocks on the metal examination table. It was cold. "Doc? Is that goddamn doctor around? I need something for the pain, Doc."

"In a minute," said Painter. "Now could you be more specific, Mr. Loney?"

"Let me think? For Christ's sake?" Ike acted disgusted. He liked this game. He had never been seriously interrogated before.

Painter stepped back and glanced at the other men. The two highway patrolmen were standing against the wall by the door. They were a couple of grim-looking customers. Their chocolate-colored coats were covered with emblems and badges. One of them wore a Western hat with a pencil roll.

Painter stroked his drooping mustache and winked at them, but neither responded. Talk about a couple of grim sonsa-bitches, thought Painter.

Quinton Doore was leaning against a file case, staring at the scale in the corner. He had a sudden desire to weigh himself officially, but he would have to let the silence pass before he could do it. His only interest in the business at hand was that they brought the old man to the reservation hospital because there was no hospital in Harlem. He'd been down at the tribal office manning the radio. When the call came in, he'd decided to wander up to check it out. The funny part of it was he'd gone to school with Jim Loney. He'd even been on the same basketball team. He'd only been a seldom-used substitute, but he was in the state championship photograph in the trophy case over at the high school. He was standing right behind Jim Loney.

"Are you ready, Mr. Loney?" It was Hanson this time.

"Oh, yeah, it's all coming back to me." Ike drew the words out, long and carefully. "Yeah, I remember now, he said something about Mission Canyon. He said something about going out there to think for a while."

"Think?"

"Yeah, he had a little item to think about."

"Is he armed?" Hanson had become brusque, as though he was tired of the old man's game.

"I guess to hell. He's got my shotgun, don't he?"

Chalk one up for the old man, thought Painter. His admiration increased.

Quinton Doore had been inching his way toward the scale, but when he heard the old man say Mission Canyon, he paused. The idea didn't dawn on him right away, but the more he thought about it, the more he understood the significance of the old man's words. "That's on the reservation," he said quietly.

The others looked at him.

"That's on the reservation," he said. "That's my jurisdiction."

One of the highway patrolmen, the one without the hat, pushed away from the wall and walked up to Ike. "Mission Canyon. Are you sure about that?"

"Sure as I'm sitting here—bleeding and in pain because that fucking doctor isn't around."

"That's that," said Hanson. He had been gotten out of bed and he wasn't anxious to pursue the matter. He knew that Doore could request assistance, but he also knew that the reservation police didn't like to have his men on the reservation.

The highway patrolmen were thinking the same thing. They were responsible only for the state highways that ran through the reservation, and there wasn't one that ran up Mission Canyon.

Ike heard the cops shuffling around as they prepared to leave. He wished he could see them. He would have loved to see their faces. "Oh, there is one other thing," he said. "I don't know if it's too important."

The shuffling stopped.

He waited for a few seconds. He didn't think twice about it. "My son killed a man." Damn, he wished he could see their faces. "Myron Pretty Weasel. In a hunting accident. Only he said it wasn't no accident, if you catch my meaning."

Ike Loney sat on the examination table. He was naked and his small drooping breasts almost reached his tight little paunch. Below the heavy gauze bandage, his lips curved into a smile and he wished he could see the faces of these so-called lawmen.

"Goddamn it!" Hanson bawled. His fat face tightened with anger. Now it wasn't just a family squabble. Now it was real trouble. And furthermore: "Old man Pretty Weasel came into the station this afternoon, said his son hadn't been home for three days. Three days!"

"Is that the basketball player?" said Painter.

"One and the same." Hanson turned to Doore. "Did you people get a report on him?"

But Quinton Doore was dialing a number. He dialed slowly, making sure. He was perched on the small desk, one foot flat on the floor, the other dangling. He was a tall scrawny man of thirty-five. He was the only person in the room, besides Ike, who didn't have a uniform on. His Levi's were faded and thin on the thigh; his Wellington boots didn't appear to have heels; and his sheepherder's coat had a big bleach spot on the forearm. He looked like any Indian man you might see walking down the highway on a winter's day. Yet there was something about his face, a kind of cruelty around the eyes, that set him apart from everybody, Indian and white. He was given to impulses at odd moments, but he was not impulsive. Those moments were serious and deliberate. "We've got a little trouble," he said into the receiver. "A shooting." He listened a moment, eyeing the scale in the corner. "No. Three days ago. Myron Pretty Weasel. That's the one. Jim Loney. His old man just told us. Hanson and Barthelme. And a couple of HP. Mission Canyon. That's where he said he was heading. I don't know. We have to check it out. I'll get Lefthand and take a run out." Quinton Doore listened for a long moment. He didn't like what he was hearing, but his expression didn't change.

Painter Barthelme watched Doore and he thought, I should be tired, exhausted, but I'm not. He glanced up at the big clock above the door. Three-thirty. Two and a half hours to go. I'm going to quit, he thought. I don't like this job. I can't deal with it. He wished that he were at home, drinking beer with the football coach, or working on one of his model planes, but most of all, being with Rhea Davis. He had made up his mind that he was going to call on her after Christmas. But now that seemed like such a long way off. He wanted desperately to be with her right at this moment. He had never in his life felt his life so isolated and barren as he did in that room full of men and the smell of medicine. Rhea Davis represented to him the safe, the civilized, side of society. Although he still hadn't talked to her in a personal way, he loved her for that and for what she would offer him—her safe, warm life.

"Well?" It was one of the highway patrolmen.

Painter jerked his head. His eyes had stuck on the clock. He was more tired than he thought. But the HP was addressing Doore.

"That was the superintendent," said Doore. "You're in."

"What about us?" Hanson tapped his chest with one hand and gestured toward Painter with the other.

Doore looked at Hanson. The superintendent had said to get all the help he could. Doore said, "You're out."

Painter almost moaned with relief, but Hanson said, "Just a darn minute here. How do you think it's going to look if we're not there? The whole ruckus started in our town. We've got to be there; otherwise it's going to look like we couldn't handle it. Some crazy bastard shoots up the town, we've got to be there!"

Doore lit a cigarette with his disposable lighter. He had owned the lighter for almost a year and it still worked. It was one of the best bargains of his life. He blew the smoke toward the scale. He was mildly irritated but he said, "Just stay out of the way."

"Damn right," said Hanson. He was breathing hard. He had never much liked Indians and he was damned if he was going to take any crap off one now. He turned to Painter. "You go with them," he said. He looked around the room, first at the highway patrolmen, then at Doore. "You're one of them now," he said to Painter. And he brushed by Ike Loney's dangling legs on his way to the door. "You're a part of this," he called back to Painter. His jacket and shirt had worked up over his roll of fat. Painter wished he were back in California. He'd have given his left nut to see a lovely wet eucalyptus tree in the hills behind Berkeley.

14

Loney turned south at the agency onto 376. It was a good highway, straight and true to the Little Rockies. The first few miles it dipped in and out of deep wide gullies that carried the spring runoff down to the Milk River valley. After that it climbed up onto the prairies and rolled gently south.

The Chevy ran well for having been driven so seldom in the past three or four months. Loney kept it at a steady 55 mph and checked the gauges, which seemed to be functioning and normal. He had the defroster opened up, but only a breath of warm air reached the windshield. The side and rear windows were thick with frost, but Loney didn't mind at all. He only needed to see straight ahead.

He was still a little surprised that his house hadn't been staked out, that he hadn't walked into a trap when he went there to get his car. It could have been all over by now, he thought, and then he put that thought away. Perhaps his father hadn't squealed, perhaps his father felt some loyalty, if not love, and this trip was all for nothing. But he knew his father was the worst type of dirt—he would squeal and he would enjoy the attention. If Loney had him pegged right, the past three hours would have given him a chance to be something. Loney felt almost sorry for the old bastard.

15

Kate sat on the window seat in the living room of her Georgetown apartment and waited for her cab. She glanced at her watch and it was almost six. She hated to catch a plane from Dulles because it was so far out of the city, but the only flight to Seattle at that hour left there. And she had to be in Seattle that afternoon in order to catch a ferry across to Bainbridge Island. She had to speak to a group of education specialists from the reservations in the area. She wouldn't have minded so much if she hadn't just got back to town the day before.

It's a miracle that I don't have an ulcer, she thought. And she thought again of the strange conversation she had heard on her answering machine. It was between her brother and a telephone operator. The operator kept trying to get her brother to leave a message and he apparently didn't know how. Now Kate wondered if he was in some kind of trouble, or if he had finally decided to come to Washington, D.C. It can't be that, she thought, it just can't be. And yet she couldn't think what else it could be. He had never tried to call her before.

She watched a pair of yellow lights cut the thick gray air down the block. She started to put her coat on, but the car swished by, turned left at the corner and started up the hill. It was a shiny foreign car and it had a left-over look about it, as though the party had just ended and it was reluctantly making its way home.

Kate walked down the hallway to the kitchen and poured herself a cup of coffee. It was warm and bitter. She checked to make sure all the burners on the stove were off, then she turned out the light and walked back to the living room. She sat on the window seat and drank her coffee. The room was austere but warm—spare Danish furniture, a couple of flokatis on the bare hardwood floor, and three framed paintings by an Indian artist she had met in South Dakota. Two of the paintings were of Indian dancers, "fancy dancers," and their movements were kinetic and exaggerated. The third was of a dancer walking home along a highway, still in full regalia but lonely and tired. The land was a series of browns and yellows leading to an ocher sky. The painting had always inspired Kate. She felt that her purpose was to create something for him to go home to. In all her years in education, she had never grown cynical about it. It had gotten her up and out of a dismal existence and she expected that it could do the same for others.

Now she wondered if that was true. She had been slowly and sadly heading toward the conclusion that it took quite an extraordinary person to make the attempt to rise above his life. Most were resigned to survival on that level of existence they were born to.

I will call Rhea from Seattle, she thought. I will leave a number where I can be reached. She will at least deliver that message. Then she thought it would be funny if they both were in Seattle right now, if things had worked out. But then a feeling of dread came over her and she knew things were not right and she felt, as she watched the fancy dancer walk home, that she would not see her brother again.

She put her cup on the ledge beside her and hugged herself. The room was cold and she rocked back and forth and hugged herself. The cab sat in the street below, its exhaust a plume that rose and dissipated in the gray light.

16

The car coasted to a stop about a quarter mile from the Hays cutoff. Loney turned off the lights and climbed out. He had the bottle of Scotch in one hand and the shotgun in the other. The wind had died completely and he could see the Little Rockies, black and silent, about three miles distant. Below the mountains he could make out the lights of Hays, and he heard a dog bark. He looked up at the sky and he had no idea of time. It had been a long night and the sky gave no indication that it was about to end.

Loney unscrewed the cap from the bottle of Scotch. Then he popped the plastic pourer out of the neck and threw it away. He took a long drink, his eyes on the mountains, and the Scotch didn't taste as good as he would have liked, but it warmed him. That was the main thing now. Stay warm. He wanted to run, but it would have been awkward with his burden, so he walked a fast pace. He took the Hays cutoff and he felt the gravel through the thin soles of his shoes.

Half an hour later he was walking through the small town and a dog was walking silently behind him. It was a rangy black dog and it was neither friendly nor unfriendly. Once Loney stopped and took a drink and the dog stopped and sat alertly waiting.

Loney decided it must be very early because all the houses were dark. And he remembered the boy who had watched him chip Swipesy out of the frozen mud and he wondered which house was his. Amos After Buffalo, and he came from "out there." Loney saw him standing on the bleak Harlem street, pointing south to these mountains and his country. That had been on Thanksgiving Day, almost a month ago. Amos After Buffalo will grow up, thought Loney, and he will discover that Thanksgiving is not meant for him. It will take him longer because he lives in Hays and Hays is on the edge of the world, but he will discover it someday and it will hurt him, a small wound when you think about it, but along with the hundred other small cuts and bruises, it will make a difference, and he will grow hard and bitter and he might do something bad, and people will say, "Didn't we tell you, he's like all the rest," and they will think Indians do not know the meaning of the word "Thanksgiving."

Amos, if I could, I would take you with me, right now, and

spare you sorrow. I might survive. Oh, God, we might survive together, and what a laugh. . . .

Loney turned to the dog. "You tell Amos that Jim Loney passed through town while he was dreaming. Don't tell him you saw me with a bottle and a gun. That wouldn't do. Give him dreams. Tell him you saw me carrying a dog and that I was taking that dog to a higher ground. He will know."

Loney was standing outside an abandoned store. Its windows had been boarded over. A faded red gas pump stood close to the door. Loney could just make out the flying red horse and he couldn't remember which gas it belonged to. The village was dark and quiet. The dog was gone.

Loney started to run. He thought he could see the sky becoming opaque and he thought he could feel a change in the air, the comfortable chill of dawn. He had a mile to go, and as he ran, he heard the Scotch sloshing wildly in its container.

When he reached the mouth of Mission Canyon, it was coming dawn and the tall gray walls seemed more a barrier than an entrance. He stopped and caught his breath and took one last look at the world. And it was the right light to see the world, halfway between dark and dawn, a good way to see things, the quiet pleasure of deciding whether the things were there or not there.

And Loney saw the dark shape of the stone mission school where it should have been and he remembered the time he had played basketball against its team. There was a small gym out back, a court not much smaller than the building, a court about three quarters the size of a normal court. The others had laughed at the priest who coached the team because he wore a long black skirt and he had a way of waggling his ass. They slaughtered the mission school and in the team bus they laughed all the way back to Harlem at the priest in the skirt. One of the players wrapped a towel around his waist and minced up and down the aisle like a fairy and everybody laughed and tried to grab him. Then they talked about sticking it to the cheerleaders who sat in the first two rows behind the driver.

Loney closed his eyes and tried to laugh at the thought of the priest in the black skirt, but he remembered Brother Gerard and there was no laughter in him, not then, not now. He was tired and his mind was full of flickering images, of scenes just past and scenes a long time past. He stood with his eyes closed and tried to black out the images, but they kept coming like dark birds, one following another, in and out of his mind, simple memories of trivial times. But they brought me here, he thought, to this place, to this time. Presently he opened his eyes and the birds were gone, and he turned and entered the canyon.

The entrance was just wide enough for a small stream and a two-track road. The creek hissed and clattered beneath a crust of snow and Loney could hear the snow break beneath his step. It was night again, but when he looked up between the looming walls he saw a narrow strip of gray light. There were no stars anymore. If it had been any other night Loney would have been a little frightened by those towering cold walls, the darkness and his step. He thought about the Indians who had used the canyon, the hunting parties, the warriors, the women who had picked chokecherries farther up. He thought of the children who had played in the stream, and the lovers. These thoughts made him comfortable and he wasn't afraid.

Twenty minutes later he reached the point where the road cut across the creek. Although the creek was only six feet wide, a distance Loney could jump with ease, the road was solid wet ice on either side. It was risky, so Loney sat down and took off his shoes and socks and rolled his pant legs up.

He waded carefully, for the creek bed at the ford was slick. His legs ached and he could feel his calves begin to knot up. He knew that he wouldn't be able to negotiate the small incline to the other side, so he waded upstream a few feet until he was off the ford. He felt the small stones beneath his feet and he took three steps and he was standing on the crusty bank. He put down the gun and the bottle and rubbed his legs. He had a cramp in his left instep and he tried to move his foot to get the circulation going. He took off his parka and wrapped it around his lower legs. Then he picked up the bottle of Scotch and drank. He stamped his foot and he moved his toes, but the cramp wouldn't go away. It was painful, so painful that he thought the bones in his foot were bending. He dropped to the ground and held his foot close and beat at the instep with his fist, trying to loosen the muscle. Whether it was the whiskey or the beating, the pain subsided a little. He put his socks and shoes on; then he stood and got into the parka. He breathed deeply and the air caught in his chest, paralyzing his body for an instant with the suddenness of the chill. He decided it must be below zero, how much didn't matter. But his skin felt warm and his feet, so cold only seconds before, now were stinging with warmth. He picked up his bottle and the gun and limped up the road.

And the canyon opened out into a small valley filled with alder, chokecherry bushes, willow and buckbrush. The ground was bare again from the few hours each day that the sun struck the meadow in the center of the valley. It had been a mild early winter, bright days and a couple of good chinooks. The snow hadn't had a chance to build up and most of the surrounding peaks were bare. Loney thought it would be a bad year for the farmers if they didn't get more snow, and then he realized that he was thinking of a future that didn't concern him. He glanced up at the sky and it was turning from gray to light blue. They could come anytime, he thought. He had figured they would wait for daybreak to hunt him down. Now he recognized a clearing beside the road as the place he had picnicked with the minister and his wife. They had had a surprisingly good time. The minister had even hit him some fly balls. It had been the only time Loney could remember that the minister had acted as if he was having a good time.

Loney looked off to his left at the ridge and he saw the rocky outcropping that he had climbed that day. It didn't seem so far away now, and it didn't appear as menacing as it had that day he climbed it and spied on the minister and his wife. They never touched in the house in Harlem, but that day Loney had caught them holding each other.

He left the road and bushwhacked his way through a stand of chokecherry bushes.

17

Painter Barthelme stood beside the car in the cold gray light. He stamped his feet and flexed his fingers. Every now and then he glanced back at the tribal office. He couldn't understand what was taking Doore so long. It seemed clear to Painter that they had to get to Mission Canyon at first light, and it was already past that. He didn't need to look at his watch. He knew it was very close to six-thirty.

Doore was a funny man. Painter was impressed with his procedure: he had the highway patrol and the Blaine and Phillips County sheriffs' people blocking off the highway at both ends of the Little Rockies. In addition, a couple of deputies were already in place in Zortman and Landusky, two villages on the other side of the mountains. The fugitive would almost have to come out at either place if he tried to cross over. So the small mountain range was sealed off. The only thing left was to flush Jim Loney. And that was the trouble. Only three of them were going in—Painter, Doore and Lefthand. How could three men hope to find one man in all that area? It would take forever and Painter wanted it all to be over. The thought had occurred to him again that he could quit anytime. He was going to quit and he could quit now. Nobody had a gun to his head. But it was important to him to clean up this loose end, to end this awful business for his own sake, to end with a little honor. He thought of the small hand-lettered sign above the radio back at the station: DO ONE THING TODAY THAT YOU DO NOT WANT TO DO.

He heard the door slam behind him and when he looked back, he saw Doore and Francis Lefthand descending the stairs. Doore had strapped on his gun and he didn't look any more official. From the way it rode on his narrow hip, Painter guessed it to be a short .38. Lefthand also had a pistol, the butt sticking out of the pocket of his blanket coat. Over his shoulder Lefthand had a rifle with a capped scope that made Painter realize they were actually going to hunt Loney.

"Hey, Barthelme, how's it going?" called Lefthand, and Painter felt a little better. He liked Lefthand, but more than that, he knew that Lefthand didn't know any more about police work than he did. He couldn't have been much over twenty-three or twenty-four. Painter had seen him a few times over in Harlem in the bars, but he never got drunk. Off duty he was just a cheerful kid who liked to rib Painter. Now they were both on the official side of the law and neither of them knew a damn thing about it. Not about this, Painter thought. Running in drunks is one thing, but this . . . He wondered how Doore felt.

But Quinton Doore was cold. He got in the car on the passenger side and he stared straight ahead. Lefthand raised his eyebrows at Painter and walked around to the driver's side. Painter got in back behind the mesh screen. He heard the *thunk* of the door locks. The seat smelled of booze.

"Sirens, flashers?" said Lefthand, after they turned out onto the highway.

"No," said Doore.

"That's right." Lefthand laughed. "Who the hell we going to encounter at this time of morning?"

But dawn wasn't far away. The sky to the east had lightened enough so that Painter was almost sure it was clear. There was no color to it yet, but neither could he see the ragged edges of clouds. He longed for the smell of dawn, but in winter in this country there was nothing but changing light. In this country. In California, in the Bay area, there was always an odor, even in winter. Sometimes it was rain, sometimes a breeze off the bay, sometimes green things—bougainvillaea, magnolia, rhododendron, a sweet dawn smell. Here, only in summer did one smell things—sagebrush, alfalfa and once in a while, from the mountains, jack pine. But the smells were never exotic, never sharp, as though it were the dust one smelled. Now Painter smelled the boozy back seat and the sour odor of his own guts and he leaned back and closed his eyes.

"How we going to go about it?" he heard Lefthand say.

"We'll go up the canyon and get him," said Doore.

"Yeah. I mean, how?"

And Painter felt himself drifting off and he smelled the brackish water at the lower end of the Bay. He saw the flats and the industries, the hillside houses beneath the roily clouds, and he thought of the girl he had met, lived with and left in Palo Alto. That had been four years ago and she had been a political science major and a part-time artist. He could barely remember what she looked like beyond the long brown hair and the pale prettiness of her face. He did remember her lithe body (they had lived together for six months) and he remembered the wild things she did with that body in wild moments. She delighted in shocking him with her imagination and her athletic ability. Now he almost laughed (as she had then). It was funny to think that those things which he had disapproved of were the very things which mildly excited him now. But it hadn't been funny then. She had called him a serious romantic because he wanted to take rides to Carmel, to make love to her in quaint motels, to sit in seaside bars and drink margaritas and think of a career beyond that of a security patrolman. But she was too immediate and worldly. She was a rich kid and she had no desire to dream. Painter could not remember the color of her eyes or whether her fingernails were long or short. That's some kind of revenge, he thought, but he had never wanted to hurt her, even when she had called him a boob and kicked him out of the house on New Year's Eve after they had played Monopoly and drunk champagne. It had been such a silly thing to do, he had left. A few months later, he quit his job and came to Harlem. Now he was quitting this job and he would probably return to California. Fuck the tundra, he said to his eyelids. He was warm and he thought of his Palo Alto girl and Rhea Davis and the smell of the brackish water of the Bay.

18

The first thing Painter saw was a boarded-up store and a gas pump with a flying red horse on its bulb. Then he heard Lefthand say, "I still think we should stop and see if St. John is around. He knows this country."

"So do I."

Painter sat up and saw the last of Hays. Then he looked through the wire mesh and he saw the Little Rockies. He had never been this close. They were bigger and wilder than they looked from Harlem. He looked straight ahead and he could see no entrance.

"Hey, there's the mission." Lefthand sounded excited but not nervous. "My cousins go there."

"What do you think?" Painter said to the back of Doore's head.

"What kind of shoes you got on?" said Doore.

Painter didn't even hear him.

19

Loney tried to remember how many shells he had left. He had used two shots, but he couldn't remember how many he had pushed up into the magazine. He looked at the magazine and he tried to estimate how many shells it held. Five? Six? Did he fill it? He must have at least a couple of shots left. He was getting drowsy. From his position on the rocky outcropping he could see down to the foot of the valley where the road forded the creek. But sometimes he forgot to look; other times he forgot what he was looking for. The ford seemed important. He drank from the green bottle and for a few minutes he was warm and in control. They were coming. Any minute now. How many? But that wasn't important. They could send the whole U.S. Army after him. It didn't matter. He rocked back and forth on his heels and the balls of his feet. The rocks were frosty and he couldn't sit down. His ass was numb. He must have frostbite of the ass by now. His foot still ached from the cold water but he only noticed it when he thought about it. Or he thought about it when it ached. He was cold clear through. He had never been this cold. He thought he should stand up and run in place. Or just run. Across the mountains. He could make it. They weren't that big. He could come out at Zortman. He could steal a car there. Zortman. Or Landusky. Landusky was a ghost town. Gold town. Which was it? Off the reservation, anyhow. Reservation used to include all the mountains until the white men discovered gold. Then they moved the reservation line north so they could dig it up. Indians didn't need it. Now everybody needed it and there was no gold. Ran out and Landusky died. A ghost town. But they never moved the line back.

Then Loney remembered his dream, the dream about the young woman who had lost her son. Again he saw her face beneath the makeup and the black shawl and it was easy this time. He did recognize her and he knew who the lost son was. She was not crazy—not now, not ever. She was a mother who was no longer a mother. She had given up her son to be free and that freedom haunted her. All the drinks, all the men in the world, could never make her free. And so she had come back to him in his dream and told him that her son would not allow himself to be found. He was not in that churchyard grave—he was out here in these mountains, waiting. And he wondered if he would be found, if he would see her again, if a heaven or hell existed. But there had to be another place where people bought each other drinks and talked quietly about their pasts, their mistakes and their small triumphs; a place where those pasts merged into one and everything was all right and it was like everything was beginning again without a past. No lost sons, no mothers searching. There had to be that place, but it was not on this earth.

Loney tried to stand but he couldn't. His legs were frozen. He looked across the valley and he saw the gold line of sunrise on the opposite mountain. Where the fuck are they? He was breathing hard and he realized that his lungs were frozen too. The harder he breathed the less air he got. And he thought of his cigarettes. But he saw the crumpled pack on the ledge five feet away. He had run out, but that didn't matter either. How could he need a cigarette? He drank some more of the

Scotch and it didn't taste like anything. Again he looked across the valley and the gold line had descended. A mountain of gold.

He heard the car before he saw it, the noise of the engine magnified by the canyon walls. It was the first sound he had heard in two hours. Then he saw the black tribal police car rolling slowly over the two-track road. It stopped on the other side of the ford and sat for a moment, its exhaust rising high above it. It must be warm in there, Loney thought, but he wasn't cold anymore. The car backed up thirty feet; then Loney heard the whine of the tires as it moved forward, picking up speed until it hit the ford. The car bounced through the water and up the incline on the other side, its tires shrieking as it neared the top; it reached the level bare ground and it shot forward, then slowed, and began to creep slowly up the valley. Loney glanced back to the narrow part of the canyon, but no other vehicles were in sight. One car. But it would do.

The car was nearing the wide place in the road. Loney's craggy perch was a couple of hundred yards from the road and about a hundred feet up. They would never see him. But he was counting on them to stop at the wide place to get their bearings.

He wondered who it would be. He knew all three of the tribal cops. He was certain that one of them would be Doore. The thought frightened him, but it interested him as well. When they were kids playing basketball, Doore had had an intensity about him, a cold hostility that made the others wary. Even Pretty Weasel. Doore had been a substitute, not very good, but in scrimmages he punished his man with a grim indifference. No one on the team liked him, and he seemed to prefer it that way. Loney had seen him several times since, but Doore had never acknowledged any familiarity. He had always been a thug. Now it seemed ironic to Loney that he was the fugitive and Doore the lawman.

The car pulled off the road and Loney pumped a shell into

the breech. He couldn't hope to reach the car from his position, but he didn't mean to. He grabbed a ledge behind him and pulled himself to his feet. Then he aimed the gun a little ahead of the car and pulled the trigger.

20

Painter heard the distant boom and he watched Doore glance out the windshield, then open his door and slide out. He knelt in the V of the open door and scanned the ridge to the east of the valley. Then Painter was squatting beside Doore and watching Lefthand dive to the ground behind them. He motioned Lefthand in close behind the car and he saw that Lefthand had his gun drawn. It was a .45 automatic. Painter had never seen a pistol that big. And he looked down and he saw his own gun in his hand. He hadn't remembered drawing it from its holster.

"See anything?" Lefthand whispered, and Painter shook his head. Doore had not moved from his position, he hadn't moved an inch, and his gaze seemed to be riveted on something on the ridge. Painter looked up—he had to look through the windshield—and he saw the small figure on an outcropping. The figure did nothing to hide or to run off. It simply stood motionless.

"Is that him?" said Painter.

Doore turned his face and grinned. "That's the great Loney."

And Painter realized what was going on. He felt stupid. All the clues were there. Loney telling his old man exactly where he was going, then making a scene at his old man's place to draw the police, then leaving his car beside the road on the other side of Hays. It was very simple: Loney wanted to be found and Doore had known this all along. That was why Doore didn't want a whole party to go into the mountains to flush Loney. Loney would be there, just as he was now. Painter read the signs, but he didn't know why Loney would do this. There are odd things that people do, he thought, things done out of a need that defies an ordinary man's reasoning. Lefthand gave him a pair of binoculars and he watched Doore take the caps off the scope mounted on the rifle. Then he watched Loney through the glasses and he recognized him. For some reason he had thought they were hunting a total stranger, a faceless stranger who had committed the act of murder. In those terms, this manhunt had been a game, the natural counteraction to the man's actions. But as he watched the man he realized that he had seen him just the other day, slipping out of the hotel and hurrying down to Kennedy's; moreover, he had seen him a few times before, once in a bar close enough to touch. In fact, they had touched shoulders, a small contact that meant nothing.

Then he heard the blast beside him and he saw the figure spin and disappear.

21

The slug spun him around and he sat down hard on a flat rock. His shoulder felt wet and cool. He looked at it and he saw the small hole in his parka, the fabric feathered and slightly funneled where the slug had entered. At first he thought that he was mistaken, that the hole had been there, and that he hadn't really been shot. But when he looked down at the bottom of his sleeve, he saw that his hand was turned outward away from his body. And when he tried to move his fingers nothing happened and he knew that his shoulder had been shattered. It was numb but curiously warm. He felt the coolness run down his arm and his brain grew tangly. He thought there was nothing in the world but that arm with the fingers turned away at an awkward curve. He watched the wristband of his parka turn dark, and then he saw the rivulet of blood break free and run down his hand to the end of his little finger. The drop clung and grew, then it fell, and he watched the blood spattering the stones.

This is what you wanted, he thought, and that was the last thought left to him. He stood and he felt a dimness in his head and he took two steps and he felt something sharp in his stomach as though someone had jabbed him with a stick. And he fell, and as he was falling he felt a harsh wind where there was none and the last thing he saw were the beating wings of a dark bird as it climbed to a distant place.